Clint Faraday Mysteries
#5
Dangerous Curves

Clint flies from Panamá City to Bocas del Toro, where a beautiful woman flirts with him. He makes a date with her for that night. Strange things start to happen around him, there is a murder – that she seems to be mixed up in, somehow

Clint Faraday Mysteries
#5
Dangerous Curves
© C. D. Moulton 2010 & 2011

About the author

CD was born in Lakeland, Florida. His education is in genetics and botany. He has traveled over much of the world, particularly when he was in music as a rock rhythm guitarist with some well-known bands in the late sixties and early seventies. He has worked as a high steel worker and as a longshoreman, clerk, orchidist, bar owner, salvage yard manager and landscaper – among other things.

CD began writing fiction in 1984 and has more than 115 books published as of this time in SciFi, murder, orchid culture and various other fields.

He now resides in Bocas del Toro and David, Panamá, where he continues research into epiphytic plants. He loves the culture of the indigenous people and counts a majority of his closer friends among that group. Several have "adopted" him as their father. He funds those he can afford through the universities where they have all excelled. "The Indios are very intelligent people, they are simply too poor (in material things and money. Culturally, they are very wealthy) to pursue higher education."

CD loves Panamá and the people. He plans to spend the rest of his life in the paradise that is Panamá

- Estrelita Suarez V.

CD is involved in research of natural cancer cure at this time. It has proven effective in all cases, so far. It is based on a plant that has been in use for thousands of years, is safe, available, and cheap. He has studied botany, and was cured of a serious lymphoma with use of the plant, *Ambrosia peruviana*.

Information about this cure is free on the FaceBook page, Ambrosia peruviana for cancer. CD asks only that all who try it please report on its effectiveness on that group.

Trash and Treasures

Afternoon Flight

It was a bit drippy/drizzly when Clint Faraday, retired detective from Florida, boarded the plane in Panamá City for the flight to Bocas Town on Isla Colón. The rain had stopped. It was going to soon turn into a nice enough day, now that he was leaving.

Well, Judi (Lum, neighbor) said it was nice in Bocas. He would get home early enough to enjoy a couple of hours of the afternoon.

He was seated just in front of the wing, window seat. Next to him was a rather attractive – well, a knockout, really – woman of about twenty six or eight years. Fantastic shape, about 5'8", reddish mahogany hair past her shoulders, green eyes, perfect teeth, even medium tan.

She smiled and said her name was Gina. Gina Halverson. She was Colombian, not a gringo, though both her parents were from the states. She was a secretary to a semi-politician, lawyer, and stock dealer, among other things. She had a job in Bocas Town that started in the morning. A stock and real estate dealer she knew from Colombia. He had worked with her father, though she didn't know him well or much about him.

Clint introduced himself, said he was a gringo – at the moment.

"At the moment?"

"As soon as I can, I'll become Panameño. I love this place."

"I can see why. It's beautiful. I really like the people, though some of them can be pains in the ass."

Clint laughed. "Yeah. Some of any people can be pains in the ass. I particularly like the Indios. They're very real people."

"I tend to like the indigenos in Colombia. They are, as you say, people who are very real. I know I'll like you. We share a philosophy. The ones who I can't stand here and anywhere else are the arrogant bigots. They too seldom have anything to be arrogant about."

"Well, seeing as we are destined to like each other, maybe I can show you around Bocas this evening?"

"*That*, I think, would be very ... pleasant."

They talked about a number of things. Clint found she agreed with him in most things. It was going to be a great evening. He could feel it.

It was as nice in Bocas as Judi had promised, Clint noted, as he disembarked. It would be a little hot – this was the tropics – but there was a steady breeze off the Caribbean, so it would be comfortable, if he didn't overdress. He helped Gina get to the Bahia, then went home, to be greeted by Judi. She said things were as she liked them. Slow and calm. Even the tourists seemed to be in a good mood.

Judi is an attractive oriental woman who has been friends with Clint since he moved next door to her, five years ago. She had been a great help in some of his cases. She was one of the four people in Panamá who knew who Manny Mathews was. (Marko Boccini, a major mafia don from the states who had moved there to escape what he was, and to raise a family who wouldn't be ashamed of how Pops made his.)

Clint told her about the strange things his last case was still turning up. She told him all the gossip from Bocas. Same old same old, except the Wild Bill had been caught and was the reason some of their friends had disappeared over the last few years. They both knew him, slightly, from seeing him around Bocas and in David and Volcan. "They've dug up five bodies, already. We knew them all."

Clint shook his head. You'd think a detective would have noticed something about him, other than his tendency to overreact to some things. If Clint had checked on him, he would have found he was wanted in the states for years.

You live and learn, then you die. Sometimes, *or* you die.

Clint told Judi about Gina. Judi said he seemed awfully focused on her. Was she going to finally turn him into a boring one-woman man? (Clint was known as a good time, but no commitments type.)

"She's half my age. I'd consider it, I think. We get along on a different level than I'm used to."

Judi laughed and shook her finger at him. "Slow down, Don Juan! You aren't in Kansas anymore, you know!"

"Thank whatever gods may be!" Clint said, and gave her the one finger salute.

Clint laid around, went through his e-mail, then got ready and went to pick up Gina, who was overdressed. He told her that would be too hot. People don't dress up for much of anything in Bocas. She sighed and said that was too much to hope for. She'd be right back! She went back inside and came out a few minutes later in a light skirt and top. She'd also undone her hair and tied it up. Her heels were gone. She had on the same kind of footwear that Clint was wearing. Sandals (Changcletas, here)

They went to El Ultima Refugio for a fantastic meal, then walked around a bit. They stopped various other places for Clint to introduce his friends. Everyone said Dave (his nutty author/musician friend) was playing at the Lemon Grass, so they went there. Dave was an ex-rock guitarist, who now did all kinds of music. All the local musicians came and went. It was a great night. While Rob was doing a couple of Dead numbers, Dave came to be introduced. He introduced Selma, a woman he had dated in the states, who was visiting. She had never been to Panamá or Bocas and was thinking of staying. It was a paradise! Dave had lived with her in Florida a bit. She could stay at his place until she decided whether she preferred Bocas, Puerto Armuelles, Chitre, David, or wherever.

"Won't that interfere with your open sex lifestyle?" Clint asked, innocently.

"No, not really. My sex life is almost nonexistent, anymore," Dave fired back.

"Oh. I thought you and Ben had a bit of a thing," Clint replied, still oh-so-innocently.

Dave wasn't going to be outdone. "And?" He was a close friend of Ben, a known gay man, as was Clint. Even though such things weren't thought much about here, Clint doubted Dave would be interested ... still?

Selma caught on. "Oh, we don't put silly limitations on each other. I have my thing, he has his. The only thing that's set in stone is that we don't either one bring something home like AIDS or a couple of others. You won't live long enough for *that* to kill you!"

They laughed about it and talked about Wild Bill a bit. He knew Dave better than he knew Clint. Dave had always said there was something a little scary about him, but what had happened was beyond anything considered. They talked about the new businesses in town (most of which would be gone in six months) and Dave went back to do a few numbers. He would be playing at Lily's, Saturday.

Clint went home. Gina went with him. She said she really liked his friends, so far. They seemed as natural as the Indios. She thought Dave was a lot better musician than you'd expect to meet in such a place.

"You wouldn't believe who comes here." He told her about a few of the people Dave played with and for back in the late sixties, such as Janis Joplin.

It was a perfect night. Clint was up at five thirty and was laying in the lounge on his deck with coffee to watch the sunrise. Gina came out and said she would fix some breakfast. What did he want?

"Hojaldres and coffee. Maybe some bolitas," Clint replied. "We can walk into town and get something at Don Chichos or Chitres."

"I make hojaldres. The coffee's made. It's sitting right there. You have ground meat for the bolitas?"

Clint told her where to find everything and said she didn't have to cook.

"Why not? I do every morning at home," she replied. "I usually don't care for the hojaldres in the cafés. They make them with too much sugar and get them too soft or too hard. Panameños use too much salt."

She even liked the same cooking as Clint!

They sat around, after the truly delicious breakfast, for a few minutes, then Clint made some chicha from a guanabana he'd bought from an Indio who came to his dock with anything special. Gina had never tasted it before. She said it was the most delicious fruit drink she'd ever tasted!

Clint began to wonder if maybe she could make a one-woman man of him! It was too good to be real! He sure as hell wasn't going to fight it.

Gina had to be at work at eight thirty, so Clint walked into town with her. She met Ben, who was a neighbor. He confided in her that he had tried to get Clint into bed for five years. He wasn't going to stop trying, just because some fantastic-looking bitch was in the way. She laughed and said to go for it, but no man would look at him, after spending an hour with her!

When they left Ben at the Hawaii Gina, said she liked his friends – even the beyond-the-normal ones.

"Beyond the normal? Like who?"

"Oh, come on, Clint! There's no way you can say Dave's norm ... well, here. The ones who are boringly normal lumps back home would be the abnormal ones here!"

"We all like to have fun. No one takes offense. We can joke about it."

She nodded. "I see that. Not much is weird or strange here."

That would soon change.

"Clint!" Judi called across the bay from her deck. "Phone!"

Clint raised an eyebrow, and went inside to call Judi.

"Something very weird is happening," she reported. "It may be connected to ... but it can't be!

"Remember that land, on the point, just below The Bluffs? With those coconuts and pineapples and yuca?"

Clint said he did.

"There was a report that there may be a body buried there, so Serg (police. Sergio Valdez) went out and used a probe in all the likely areas.

"They didn't find a body. They found a treasure chest. Lots of gold and emeralds and such. Doubloons and crucifixes and the regular things. It was a large chest, I understand."

"It isn't the first pirate treasure found around here," Clint pointed out.

"And about a million and a half in dollars. That kind of thing was found around here, too, but not in the same box!

"You never turn your phone on. Serg wants you to come out. You can take the boat."

Clint looked at his phone. It was on, but on silent ring mode. He sighed and said he'd go. She said to pick her up. This, she had to see.

He called Sergio on his private celular. He said there were some things Clint would find very interesting in the chest. It was also interesting that there was such a call that would lead them to this kind of thing. He couldn't trace who had made the call. Gloria thinks it was a woman, but she's not sure. They hung up too soon.

Clint said he'd be there in twenty minutes, then called Manolo, an interpol agent (No one but Clint and a couple of friends knew that), to ask if he had a clue. Nothing.

Clint picked Judi up at her dock and headed for the point, then to where he could see the police and a bunch of gawkers. He beached the boat and walked over to look at the chest.

It was definitely an old chest. It was covered in copper that was almost oxidized through, in spots. It was about four feet by two and maybe twenty inches deep. The jewelry and such was certainly authentic. The stacks of hundred dollar bills looked real, to Clint.

"Judging by the series on the bills, this has been here about fifty years," Sergio said.. Clint shook his head.

"There's something on a few of the bands on the money. B. B. y H. H. Mean anything?" He showed a band to Clint. It was in marker, hand written. Clint shook his head.

This was weird. Surely no one who knew about that kind of treasure would report it to the police! They could get every bit of it and be gone before anyone knew about it. They could dig it up, clean out the chest, and rebury it and no one would know. It would be a truly rare accident for anyone to be where they could see what was going on, there. It was hidden enough that regular traffic on the Caribbean wouldn't see them there. His only clue was some initials or a code or something.

He talked with a few people, then said he was going back. Judi said there wasn't anything that struck her.

Silvio Guerra, an Indio friend, caught Clint's eye and motioned with his head. Clint mouthed "Casa?" and Silvio nodded. Silvio had a small place just past The Bluffs, going toward Bocas Town.

Clint and Judi headed back home.

"Que paso?" Clint greeted Silvio.

"Ola, Clint. (Rest translated) I thought I would tell you that there was someone where they found the treasure last night. A woman, I think. She was there just when the moon came up over Carenero. She had a machine like they use on the beach to find money."

"A metal detector?

"The moon isn't far past full, so it was about eight thirty or nine. Did she come by boat?"

"I did not see. I don't ... she ... I was in my cayuca, coming back from Drago. I think ... maybe there was a small ... one of those jet ski things."

"Oh. Then from Bocas," Clint replied.

"They have them at the Playa Mango and some of those places," Silvio pointed out. Clint nodded and thanked him, then went back toward his house.

A woman. From Bocas. On a jet ski or PWC. He went into Bocas to ask around the places those were available to find none were out past about six the night before. He got on his motorcycle and rode out to several of the hotels that had jet skis and PWC's for their guests (rented at ridiculous prices, but, if you could spend 125 bucks per night, you could afford 50 for a jet ski for an hour). The only possibility was at Caracol. Three of the personal cabins on the water had PWC's.

Donald Ferguson and family, from New Jersey, Betina Blakley, from Houston, and Frank Glissom, from Atlanta. Nothing rang a bell. A call to Manolo told him none of them were on a watch list. A call to Manny resulted in nothing further.

One of those three was implicated. He would have to opt for Betina Blakley. The 'B. B.' on those bands. He didn't have another hint of a clue.

Betina Blakley stayed in her cabin, alone. No one noted when she was or wasn't there, unless she left a message to tell someone where she was.

"She did that?" Clint asked.

"We don't answer questions about the guests, here!" Nick, the manager, snapped.

"I'll be back with the police. You can explain why they were here," Clint said. "About an hour. Right at dinnertime. We'll look for you in the restaurant about then?"

He sighed. "What do you want to know?"

"If she left any messages for anyone, and who. Not content, unless it was criminal."

He went to a spike with notes on it and went through them. "She left a message for anyone twice that merely said she was going to Drago for the day and one to a Raul Avenidas, saying she would come to the office about four. Today."

"Thanks. Not much there. Certainly not criminal. I hope I won't have to bother you again."

He called Manolo and asked about a Raul Avenidas. There was a pause for about thirty seconds, then Manolo said it was possible he was being watched for jewel theft. He seemed to have a source of antiques that wasn't explained, though, so far as they knew, none of it was stolen. It was from some years ago, not recent.

Clint told him about the chest. He was very interested, but would play it quietly. He couldn't figure what it was, except that Avenidas might have found the chest and had been letting items out a little at a time.

"For how long? Fifty years?" Clint asked.

"No. He's only been at it for about twelve years. He's in his early forties."

Clint thanked him, then headed for the police station. He asked Sergio to check out Raul Avenidas, very thoroughly. They might have a break. He then went home, got a call from Gina, and prepared to take her to a few places. She wanted to try the food at The Lemon Grass, so they would start there.

They chatted a bit about her work day. She went to the hotel and changed while Clint talked with people he knew on the verandah.

"I had a good enough day, I guess. It's mostly sitting around and answering the phone," Gina said, as they strolled toward The Lemon Grass. "Only one person came into the office. A woman who wants to invest in something or other. The boss was fawning all over her. It was mostly kind of boring. The only thing that makes it a good thing is that I have the total night to do as I please.

"How was your day?"

"Other than being a little strange, pretty much the normal way of things. They found a treasure chest that had stuff hundreds of years old. Lots of gold and emeralds and such."

"I'd think that was exciting! It must be pirate treasure. I heard they found a few of them along here and in Colón."

"It was partly pirate treasure and partly cash. Dollars."

"Dollars? They didn't have dollars back in ... I guess maybe they did. The later part of the pirate problem, anyhow. Confederate money and like that."

"They were dollars from about fifty years ago."

She seemed shocked. "That doesn't make any sense!"

"My sentiments, exactly. Weird," Clint said. "Here's The Lemon Grass and this is Judi Lum, my neighbor, friend and partner in solving crime. Judi, Gina."

"I was just leaving," Judi said. "Clint told me a lot about you, Gina. I see he wasn't exaggerating, at all! Selma said you were a bit of Okay."

"It's all lies! They hate me! They're just trying to cause me grief!" Gina cried. Judi laughed and said Gina was going to be a buddy, sure as sunset.

She and Clint went in. They chatted about anything that came up. Clint introduced Gina to a dozen or so of the regular crowd. As they were leaving, a rather fat individual came in with a local "lady" who worked the bars. Gina gave him a disgusted look and hurried Clint out as the man caught a glimpse of her. He was about to call to her, but they were out. She made it a point not to look in his direction.

"Who was that?" Clint asked.

"My boss. Raul Avenidas. He's a scumbag – but he pays well. For the office. I doubt that one costs much. A few drinks and five dollars. He was nothing like I expected."

Clint laughed. Very interesting. Raul Avenidas. Betina Blakley.

They went to The Rip Tide for a few drinks and conversation with a number of people, then went to Clint's place. He suggested she move in. No need to pay for a hotel when she didn't even use the place. She said she'd consider it.

They chatted a bit and sat together on the deck. The police boat went by and several of the officers waved to Clint.

"I still wonder why there were any dollars in the chest you told me about. Do you suppose someone found it and buried it back so they could come after it later?

Maybe didn't realize they'd dropped any money in it?" she asked. "Pirate treasure should be only that! It ruins the fantasy if there are newer things in it, not to mention how it needs explanation."

"They didn't just drop the dollars in it. They put them in," Clint replied. "You don't accidentally drop a million and a half in hundreds into a box with five times that in gold and jewels already inside."

"GUHH! *Million*!?"

"Uh-huh."

She seemed to be unable to believe that. Clint wasn't so sure he could believe it. It was just plain weird.

They were in bed for about an hour when the phone rang. Clint said he'd forgotten to turn the damned thing off. He picked it up. It was Sergio.

"Clint? I'm sorry to bother you at this time of night, but there's been a murder."

"Details?"

"A woman was stabbed to death. Stabbed repeatedly. This was a murder by a person who was angered beyond control. The woman isn't from around here and knew very few people in the area, it seems. Gringa from Colombia. Fifty one years old. She was staying at Caracol, so she wasn't poor, by any standard."

"Caracol? Tell me her name wasn't Betina Blakley?" Clint said. Gina sat up and make a little cry.

"Yes. You knew her?"

"I think she was the B. B. on those bands. Any reason to come there?"

"Not that I can see."

"I'll see you in the morning, then."

"Gina, what's the matter?"

"Betina Blakley was the woman who came to the office today ... yesterday."

"Judi, this is getting weirder and weirder," Clint complained, over breakfast in the morning. Gina had made omelettes and a fruit salad. She had fallen in love with the coffee Clint had from the friend near Enel Fortuna who ground just a hint of cacao in as he ground the coffee that he grew. It was delicious.

"It really shook me when Clint said it was this Betina woman who was killed. She was in the office yesterday to talk with my boss. I figured she had money. He was fawning all over her. He can be downright obsequious," Gina said. "I pretended I didn't see him last night at The Lemon Grass, so he'll be trying to find out if I know about his whore – like I would even care.

"Clint, I'm going to wait awhile before I move in (Judi raised an eyebrow at Clint). I want to know if I even have a job, much longer. My work card isn't good for working anywhere else or for anyone else. I don't know enough to make any plans, though I'll definitely want to be back here, regardless. I like it better than Colombia."

"What part of Colombia?" Judi asked.

"Not far from Cartagena, but that's just for the work. My home, until the folks died, was near Medellin."

Judi nodded. Gina had to get to work. Clint was going to be checking a few things out. He walked Gina to work. She had to fish around for her keys because Avenidas wasn't there yet. Unusual. He was generally early. When she was inside, Clint went to Don Chichos for the gossip, then to the Golden Grill. The talk was all about the chest, very little about the murder. They didn't know much about it.

He then went to the police station to talk with Sergio, who said he had checked Raul Avenida out and hadn't learned much. The murder took his attention. It seemed he was on the fringe of a lot of sordid things, but there was never a direct connection to anything illegal. He did come up with a few articles from twelve to four or five years ago that very well could have come from that chest. He had been living on the proceeds from that, comfortably, even extravagantly, until lately. Now, it seemed his funds were getting low. His business deals certainly didn't account for what he was spending. The Blakley woman seemed to have some connection with him in Colombia and met with him twice that he knew about, in Bocas Town, over the past week. That was, apparently, from the papers in her room, about purchasing some kind of company in Colombia. He started it there, moved here, and she was only here to finalize the deal.

"Finalize a deal in Colombia in Bocas?" Clint asked. Sergio shrugged and said it probably had to do with the offshore account she had here in Panamá. "What I see at this point is that she's dead and he was the only one who knew her. That makes a couple of very important implications."

"What time was she killed?" Clint asked.

"Between ten and eleven. Closer to eleven. Out by sixth street. No one saw or heard anything."

"I know where he was at about eight thirty. The Lemon Grass. He was with a local pro. I think she calls herself Evette," Cliff said. "Not among the better ones."

"She hangs around the Submarine Sandwich place, so we can run over and talk to her," Sergio suggested. "She's probably going to be his alibi, even though I doubt he did it."

They went to the café, but she was over by the Bocas Market. They found her there. She said Raul was a bit of a weirdo, talking about the other women he knew and how they were all alike. Out to screw him out of as much money as they could.

"He really got weird about the old treasure chest they found, you know, the pirate chest, had ten million dollars in cash in it, if you can believe the word going around."

"Weird? What do you mean?" Sergio asked.

"Oh, I don't know, really. I don't speak much English and he was yelling about some cheap pig who cost him lots of money. She screwed him and he didn't even get a kiss out of it. It didn't make any sense."

"What time did you leave him?" Clint asked.

"I think it was around midnight. He said it was time to get home. He had a lot of work for today and it was already after midnight."

"You don't know for certain?" Sergio asked.

"Well, no. We were at the VIP and were a bit drunk and he left me some money. I stayed until almost closing time. Donaldo took me home."

They thanked her. Sergio asked Clint what he thought.

"We don't know a thing more than when we found her. He could have been there until midnight or he could have gotten her drunk and left at ten. She wouldn't remember."

"What I'm thinking is that the VIP is right there. Someone going down to sixth street for a taxi would pass right in front of the VIP," Sergio said. "It seems a bit convenient."

Clint nodded. It did that! "Shall we go see if his story matches?"

It was Sergio's turn to nod. They walked to the office and greeted Gina. Gina said he had come in less than five minutes ago. He had one hell of a hangover. She called on the intercom and he said to come on in, but they had to take him as they found him. It wasn't pretty.

He greeted them with, "Do *not* drink wine with dinner, beer after, then rum and tequila after that. I ended up in some dive with an ugly cheap whore I thought I'd never get rid of. Luckily, I was in a place where they knew her, so I was able to get away by buying her a few more drinks and giving the bartender ten to see she didn't leave for fifteen minutes. That's my complaint and I feel like complaining. So there!

"What can I do for you?"

"You had business dealings with a Betina Blakley?" Sergio asked.

"Oh. The Blakley woman. A real pain in the ass, but I'm going to get a big commission, so I try to be nice to her," he said. "I don't think she has anything to cause the cops to come. It's not my fault MisCamCo isn't thrilled about her getting such a block of stock, but they put it on the market, themselves. They paid their two bucks and placed their bet, far as I'm concerned. She might not have gotten her millions exactly legitimately, but that's no concern of mine, either."

"Did you know she's dead?" Clint asked.

Avenidas stared at him a few seconds, then sat down hard, almost breaking the seat off his chair. He groaned and wailed, "Then there goes my commission! I can't *afford* to lose that! Oh, *shit*! I was counting on that to ... oh, *shit fire*!

"Er, what happened?"

"She was murdered," Sergio replied. "Stabbed. Rather sadistically. Messy and bloody."

"When? She was here yesterday. She was ... she acted normally, for her. A bit nasty."

"Last night," Sergio answered. "We were wondering if she said anything to you that would indicate she was afraid of anyone, or if she acted nervous or whatever."

"Well, she was a little worried about the people who definitely did *not* want her to get control of the company, but they wouldn't go that far. No matter what else, it would solve their financial situation and let them come back fairly strongly. It would have a negative impact on them to not have the deal go through – as I very carefully explained to her.

"She always carried a lot of cash around. Was it robbery?"

"Definitely not. It was supposed to look like it, but it was definitely not robbery," Sergio said. "Her money and watch were gone, but she had on a diamond and ruby ring worth in excess of ten thousand dollars, with matching earrings worth as much, plus an antique emerald necklace that would probably bring half a million or more. I was surprised the ones who found the body didn't take them. I was even more surprised that anyone would wear that kind of stuff in Bocas, then wander around sixth street, of all places."

"I can see why they grabbed the watch. It was worth a bundle," he said. "Maybe they were about to be seen and ran. She had some kind of thing about wearing thousands of dollars worth of jewels. Flaunting that she was a rich bitch."

"Her body was found more than half an hour after she was killed, so that isn't likely," Sergio replied. "Well, we'd better get on with it. We do have the reputation for solving murders fairly quickly and positively here – until this Bill character, but we didn't really have a clue about that."

"We have the added advantage of the watch. It's damned easy to identify," Clint added. "They can't get rid of it and they damned well can't keep it. If they toss it, it'll be found, then they will."

"If they toss it they'll be found?" he asked, confused.

"Very few know about it – so don't let on. It will have to be someone we've mentioned it to," Sergio said. "We'll be in touch if we need anything more."

They went out. Gina pointed to the intercom, and grinned. Clint raised an eyebrow. He hadn't seen any indicator light on in that office.

Gina saw his look and said, "I think the little red light is burnt out or something." He grinned again. He told her to keep her ears open, but don't go too far. One person was already dead.

They went to the station, where Sergio was handed several sheets of legal paper. He signed a couple, told Edith to arrest those two, then read over the next one. He said it was about Betina Blakley. She was born in Houston, Texas, and was taken to Colombia when she was less than a year old, was raised in Colombia and the states, went to UT, got an advanced degree in business administration when she was twenty two, then moved back to Colombia, where her parents were living in a small puebla near Medillin. She worked for a couple of companies, married a rich Colombian who was killed twelve years ago in a drug cartel fight. She lived by investing a lot of cash in failing companies, taking over, and making them pay. She threw a lot of money around, but she had so much she could show was legal that she was left alone. Adding up her accounts, particularly the three offshore accounts in Panamá and subtracting what she could show was legit left her with almost a hundred million, unexplained.

Not much, and a lot, at the same time, depending on how you looked at it. A little nag started in Clint's mind, but he didn't have a clue as to what his subconscious had seen.

Next page was a list of people she had been known to have had dealings with. Avenidas was one of them. She knew him a lot longer than he had let on, though he didn't seem to have had much dealings with her and it was a matter of how long, not how often. Contact between them was rare. A note said that he was in on a couple of deals with her father.

It clicked. Her father was killed twelve years ago and he had sold some jewels from that chest twelve years ago, then Betina went to where that chest was found the night before it was found – because of a tip from a woman.

That didn't make much sense. It wouldn't until he had some more to work with. It didn't make sense, anymore than that cash in the chest made sense. If that chest was dug up twelve years ago and the jewels were taken ... but the money was no newer than fifty years old. This was weirder and weirder.

"What world were you in then?" Sergio asked.

"Oogy-googy land, I think. This is one hell of a mixed mess! *Nothing* makes any sense!"

"At least you have things that make no sense. All I have is a body and one definite suspect."

"Why would he kill ... because of the cash. It wasn't supposed ... she ... I'll be damned! That fits! She didn't know the cash was in there *either*!"

"Give!" Sergio demanded.

"I just have an idea that makes partial sense. I have to know about Avenidas and her father. I have to know a hell of a lot more about what was happening twelve and fifty years ago."

"This is getting interesting ... I mean, in addition to weird."

"We didn't go too deeply into Avenidas in Colombia. There's not a lot of cooperation."

"I'll get help from Manolo and another friend," Clint promised.

Clint called Manolo for some information on Avenidas' father and Blakley Sr. Anything. Manolo could get information from Colombia that regular processes couldn't. He then called Manny to ask for any information from the states, particularly Houston, on possible connections, there. He then decided to go out to the Zapatillas to laze around and think. He got back just before five and went directly to his comp. Both Manny and Manolo would e-mail their information.

Manny had very little about Avenidas. He had probably been in the states only once and had stopped in Houston for about two hours, then gone to New York, then returned to Colombia, then back to Bocas. The office had been there for some years, but mostly as a drop address for the stock deals and a little real estate business.

Betina Blakley spent quite some time in Houston, for a number of years, but seldom in the past twenty four years. She had friends and a few business acquaintances there. There was a list of names she had most contact with.

Friends; Dona Forbes, Frieda Gormann, Glen Langefield, Helen Venders, Rebecca Venders, Louise Giotti, Frank Bendetti, Charlene Dancy, Jim Bunch. Business; Samuel Levant, Shirley Green, Harold Halverson, Josephina Cortez, Sharon Mills. Nothing rang a particular bell. Each of the listed people had short profiles. Bendetti was a bit of a wannabe thug, Green was into loan sharking, in a small way, Halverson was a contact in Colombia as well as the states. Cortez and Mills were just minor players in a restaurant and bar business.

Clint got a bit of a chill at one name. Was Halverson Gina's father or uncle?

H H y B B. That was a little scary. Gina?

She was with him. She didn't find any chest or kill anyone – but was she somehow connected to these people?

He would wait for Manolo's report.

Bernard Blakley, her father, had died in a suspicious fire in October of 1998. He had a lot of dealings with everyone and was suspected of laundering money for certain drug cartels. He had a few legit deals, but his wealth seemed to be because he was clever about manipulating stocks to where he could do a hostile takeover of a company in trouble. Not much else was known about him.

That twelve years that kept coming up was beginning to make Clint wonder. He went into town. Ben and Judi were talking in front of Ben's place, so they joined him. They met Dave at the Golden Grill, then went to the Bahia and talked Gina into going with them to The Gran Muralla Chinese restaurante for a delicious meal. Gina noted that Clint seemed to be in another world.

"I'm finding out a lot about Avenidas and Blakley," he said, deciding it would have to come out, sooner or later. Might as well make it now. "Seems they both knew your father for years."

"Raul did. A little. I mentioned that when I told you why I was coming here," she answered. "I don't know much about his dealings. Blakley might have known him. She looked just slightly familiar. I might have seen her with Father, years ago.

"Father was into some pretty shady things. I think he did some work for the drug people. He was scared of something for a couple of months before he and Mother died. He said that it was business and that Mother and I were better off not knowing. It was something that had put him into notice – he called it that – of a big drug lord named Ochoa. He died and left everything to my

Mother, who died at the same time, leaving everything to him in her will. I got everything, as surviving heir, but we haven't been able to find anything except the house and a bank account that was just more than twenty thousand dollars, US. I've managed to go through that and had to get a job or get married, which is the Colombian girl's only way to security.

"I don't want to get married, yet. I was offered a job by Raul at a time I needed it, so here I am."

"How did your parents die?" Judi asked.

"They were on their way to Bogotá and ran off the mountain when a truck was coming down the road on the wrong side. Its brakes had failed and the driver was in the hospital for four months because of being hurt when the truck went into the side of the mountain farther down.

"It was real. It wasn't a setup or murder. I had that checked out very thoroughly. It happened in September of ninety eight and was investigated completely.

"I thought, then, and still do, that Father had a lot of money tied up, somewhere. I know I saw him with big sacks of money, several times. I was in the garden one time when a man gave him a sack of money so heavy he could hardly carry it. He put it in the bodega and I snuck in to see when he and Mother went to shop. It was hundred dollar bills. I couldn't guess at how much, but it had to be a million dollars. The next day another man came and collected the sack and left.

"I was eleven years old. I didn't think much about it. Father always said Mother and I were not to concern ourselves about business things. Ever. It was the father's job to provide for the family and the mother's job to care for the house and family. They were separate parts of why a marriage worked. We got lectures on our proper roles. He was very good to us. Mother said a thousand times that he was a better provider and more caring than any other man in Colombia. I never once questioned anything he did. Looking back, I can see where maybe I should have.

"You can see why I'm so ... confused and worried about what's happened here. Raul and Blakley, then that money in a chest full of jewels. Avenidas once showed me a sword with fifteen jewels he said was very old and worth probably a million dollars. He was mixed up with Father in business. I saw millions of dollars in cash kept in sacks. Money ended up in the pirate chest, which seemed to throw Raul into a rage. Blakley was wearing some jewelry when she was killed that could have come from that chest.

"I don't know how any of it's connected. I wonder if ... I don't even know what to wonder about.

"That's my true story. I can't believe how naive I was. I never added two and two because I guess I didn't want to rock the boat."

"I'll jump to a few conclusions myself!" Judi cried. "If you weren't so naive, you'd probably be dead. Maybe Raul has you here where he can watch you because that money and chest might belong to you!"

"Yeah," Dave added. "Have the good sense not to wonder about it until Clint finds out a few things."

"This gets weirder and weirder," Clint said.

"You keep saying that," Judi said. "Let's drop it for tonight, Okay?"

Dave and Ben went to The Plank a little later. Judi, Clint and Gina went to The Toro Loco. Judi met a good friend and stayed there when Clint and Gina went to The Rip Tide to talk with Neil and Cathi. The rest of the night was very pleasant. Gina stayed at the hotel, which was the only sour note to Clint. He stopped at some little bar for a beer on his way home, where he talked to some people, but didn't even finish the beer. It wasn't going to be as pleasant a night as the last couple had been. He was a little fuzzy about the later part. He didn't think he'd had *that* much to drink.

Okay. That was possibly a very important fact. Gina's parents had died in September of '98, definitely not murdered, then Blakley died in October, as definitely murdered. Avenidas started selling antique pirate treasure in ... exactly when? He had to know that date. It was either vastly important or incidental. Nothing between.

When he got up to a dark drizzle, he checked the comp to find Manolo had sent some information. Much of it was covered by Manny's information. Blakley had been laundering for two major cartels and was trusted by them. He was knocked over, but *not* by them. They lost a few million because of that and had tried to find who and why. They weren't good at investigation. They always ordered people to talk and they talked. It wasn't always accurate information, though it was too often acted upon as though it was.

Halverson was a sort of placement man. He took the money from one place and put it in another, from which he arranged for it to go to a third place, minus commissions and fees, before returning to the original sparkling clean. His fees were reputed to have made him something over ten million dollars a year for some years. There was talk that some of it was missing at his death, that he had been ripped off for a lot more and that Blakley and some stockbroker were the ones ripping him off.

He had once put a lot of money in a treasure hunt, a lot like those things in Florida. There was a hint that something was found – because a few pieces showed up. It seemed to stop when he died, except for three pieces that showed up five years ago. There might be hundreds of millions still hidden somewhere.

Avenidas, the information was mostly what he had. He had sold the artifacts in late '97 and early '98 that they could say definitely came from him.

Clint sat back and thought. He was building a scenario that may be a mile away from the facts for every dollar in that chest.

Blakley and Halverson had a sort of semi-partnership deal in money laundering. They became rich with it. Halverson had financed a treasure hunt that had paid off. He wanted a way to keep the find safe until he could dispose of it. He had let Blakley in on it and Blakley had gone with him to see what there was to see. Fifty years ago, there was nothing and very few people on Isla Colón. They decided to keep a bit of the cash they had with the treasure as insurance against bad times. Everything was according to plan for quite a while. They both had plenty of money. They didn't need the treasure or the cash they had hidden. They let it lay.

Then the Halversons died. Now where did it go? That part was probably fairly close.

Okay. Halversons are dead, so ... Gina would inherit everything. There were maps or something left for her to find. Blakley found it first. That was why there were no notes or registrations or such for the offshore accounts. Blakley stole them from Gina.

How?

Gina was about 15 years old – and was back in the states, going to school! Blakley simply went into the house and took whatever he wanted.

How was Avenidas involved in that? How did he know about the treasure? How did he get the items?

Halverson had financed a treasure hunt. Avenidas was the stockbroker who reputedly ripped him off. That would fit. Avenidas didn't know where the treasure was, he simply had some items Blakley gave him, probably as a payoff to keep quiet. Avenidas did *not* kill Blakley. He would lose his final chance at the treasure, that way. He didn't know how to find it.

So – who did kill him? It would be whoever ended up with the treasure, which was Betina.

Another supposition. Blakley got those maps and papers and took them home. Betina found them. She knocked her old man off, herself. That would fit very nicely, thank you very much!

Now Avenidas was really in a fix. The money from the sale of the artifacts wouldn't last forever. He had no clue as to where the stuff was. He didn't have access to those offshore accounts. He was about to end up with an empty basket. What could he do?

He could see that Betina was throwing money she couldn't have around like she had a never-ending supply. Watch her! Sooner or later, she would go after the treasure.

She came to Bocas. He'd had an office there for years. He came to Bocas. He brought Gina over because ... he had something that gave her rights to that treasure. She could collect fifty percent of its value by turning it over to Panamá. He was the stockbroker who had arranged financing, so could charge her twenty percent. Twenty percent of millions was a lot of money.

He wouldn't have killed Betina, then. She had to lead him ... but the treasure was already gone! Someone had made an anonymous call about a body buried where the chest was.

Betina was going to claim rights and get half? What happened ... except that there was ... no. The chest was already found when she was killed. What had happened that made it necessary to get rid of her?

The cash in the chest! It was added to that chest before Betina was ten years old. She couldn't claim the treasure without explaining the cash. She couldn't explain the cash, which wasn't too difficult to get around – but she couldn't hope to explain why she knew about the chest. She had come here before Avenidas and was already acting suspiciously, so a claim of not knowing about it would fail.

It looked like a rage killing. It was!

Now. How to get Avenidas?

He had to learn a lot more about Avenidas and Blakley. He had what was needed for Halverson. Halverson was the type who accepted the total responsibility for his family. The family very obviously almost worshiped him. He was a very good father, if not much else.

What about Blakley? Was he a good father?

Clint could assume he was not. She wouldn't have killed him, if he was. He called Manolo and asked if he could find details on Blakley as a family man. Manolo said he had that, but didn't include it. H e didn't think it was the kind of information Clint could use to any purpose.

"You don't know!" Clint replied. "This is a weird mess. That might be behind a good part of it."

"His wife left him shortly after Betina was born. She ran away with a guy she claimed was at least a man, not a cheating snake in the grass. She wasn't any prize. She left Betina with him when the kid was less than a year old. She was raised by nannies, several of whom said he was a real monster. When he died, she actually said she would give whoever planted him a million dollars reward. She spent her life hating men. She said she was going to use all that money he got to make more. She had learned that from him.

"In other words, he would never make husband and father of the year."

"You know she killed him?" Clint asked.

"I suspect she paid someone to do it."

"I think she did it."

"I damned well wouldn't be surprised."

"Thanks, Manolo. I owe you one."

They chatted a few minutes, then Clint sat back, shook his head, sighed and went to his computer. He had to find a way to connect it to Avenidas, if only because, that way, Gina might get something out of it. Regardless of what happened later, her father found the treasure. She didn't have a clue as to what was going on. She was only nine or ten years old, so couldn't be held responsible in any way. She obviously didn't know anything about any treasure chest and she as obviously had no least idea concerning the cash in that chest.

Betina had all the secrets, but she was now out of the equation. For the future. She was most of the equation until she ended up cut to ribbons.

Nice scenario. Too bad it only fit in pieces. Something was missing from the equation. Something big. Clint was sure Raul Avenidas killed Betina Blakley. Everything else almost fit. Like a .357 shell in a .38. It worked, but there was a slight misfit. It would throw a lot of residue. The aim would be off just a bit.

Why that comparison in his mind? He just couldn't focus and seemed to be making up silly fantasies. What was damned certain was that *something* was missing. There was someone else involved. Someone who was very good at being invisible. They left footprints, even if you didn't see them go by.

If this stupid mood didn't break, he wouldn't solve anything. His mind seemed locked onto a circular track.

There was too much he didn't know. He was letting his own emotions get in the way of strict rationality.

The phone rang. He picked it up. Judi asked him what the hell was wrong with him after one minute of conversation. He told her he couldn't get his mind into gear and laid out what he was thinking, in brief.

"Clint? I know you don't use drugs, but you're acting like you're on methamphet or crack!" She sounded strange. "What have you.... Clint, what's wrong? Really?"

"Judi, I don't know! I have a headache – which I never do – and can't focus." He stretched, and looked at the comp. The clock said 10:14.

"My god! What time do you have?"

"Time? Around a quarter after ten. Why?"

"I haven't been up for a half hour! I never sleep past five thirty! It was dark and raining. I ... Judi, something IS wrong!"

"What time did you get home? What did you have to eat or drink?"

Clint tried to think. He remembered coming home, in a displaced sort of way. He had stopped at ... he couldn't remember the bar. He had talked with ... someone. He was confused as to who or what they had talked about.

"Judi, this is weirder than ever. I think I was drugged! Why? Who? I only had a beer. Nothing else."

"You usually have a tequila at Neil's. Why a beer?"

"It wasn't at Neil's. I stopped at a bar on the way home. Gina went back to the hotel and I was down, because of that. Someone was there and waved for me to come in, so I ... no. There was someone or something in the road. I was waved down ... it would have to be someone I recognized or I would have waved and gone on. I can't remember who it was! I can't remember which bar."

"Stop trying. It may come to you. You'll see or hear something that'll remind you. Association works, a lot of the time, with that kind of thing. You might have been told to forget."

"I think I was. I remember someone saying it would not be a good idea to ... something."

"Get Sergio to have you tested for scopolamine. It sounds like you were given a hypnotic, for some reason."

Clint agreed. He would go get tested. He headed for the hospital. In a taxi.

"Serg, Clint was given scopolamine last night on his way home," Judi explained. "We want to find which bar it was and who it was he saw there. They'll answer you, where they would look blank and say he wasn't there and didn't talk to anyone, if we asked."

He grimaced and agreed. He took the police truck and Clint and Judi to stop at all the bars between The Rip Tide and his house. It was the fourth one, a little local place. The old man who ran the place said Clint came in with a man and woman. She was about forty, may have been a Tica. He was a gringo. He said Clint had stopped to help him start his car and he wanted to buy him a drink. Clint ordered a Balboa and they talked for about half an hour at the little table in front.

Clint cried, "I remember stopping to help someone with a stalled truck! His name was ... George? Something like... I don't remember any woman.

"Someone came by in ... on a bike. A Ho Fai. I remember that. I was sitting at the table and he went by. I can't ... there was a woman who came from around back. She sat and was drinking a rum and coke. It was already there, so she was ... now it's gone again.

"I'd recognize George. She's a blur. It was Carlos Ramirez on the bike. He saw me and will remember the woman."

Sergio thanked the prop and they headed out toward the Bluffs. Carlos had a few hectares out there. Carlos said he didn't know who the man and woman were, but he'd seen them around. He drove a Toyota truck. Green and black with a yellow band on the doors.

"John Brandon. The woman is his wife, Sylvia. She's a Tica," Sergio said.

They thanked Carlos and headed out toward Drago to John and Sylvia's place. No one was around. A neighbor said they went to Costa Rica, early in the morning. They'd be back in four days. It was for the passport visa renewal. That left everything up in the air, for the moment. Clint was thinking a lot better, now, so would try to find who was connected with the Brandons – and if it had anything to do with the chest and murder. Sergio drove them back and said he was working on an angle he'd uncovered where Avenidas was concerned. It seemed he had tried to buy a lot of land on the coast on the other side of the Bluffs.

"So. He knew it was in that general area, but not where," Clint said. "No one had any real information, except Blakley. Now she's dead. All of these people are in big trouble with someone – but who?"

"This mean this crap doesn't stop when we tag Avenidas, doesn't it?" Sergio asked.

"It looks that way," Clint agreed.

Clint called Manny and asked if he could find out anything about John and Sylvia Brandon. He said he'd check them out. He called Manolo to see if he could find a connection. He called Judi and asked if she could check out Sylvia any way.

"I already asked some people about her," Judi replied. "It seems she was from Colombia, not Costa Rica. She just goes with John when he gets his visa updated. She has a two year visa on some kind of work card. That would mean she works for John. She's not his wife. They let people think she is. They have that place – or John does – for the past two years, but almost never come here.

"They asked a lot of questions about Avenidas, at first. John said he might want to invest in stocks. Was he trustworthy, and such. They seem to keep an eye on him and on who goes to that office. When Avenidas is here, they sit in the Seahorse Café across the street from the office for hours. They don't go there when he's not around. *Duh*!

"A little note. They were in town until after midnight night before last. I'd say you have another suspect or two."

"You're a jewel! Thanks, Judi. You get more information faster than I can. You're a damned good detective."

"I guess. For this kind of thing. I can get the information, I just don't know what to do with it when I do."

They chatted for a few more minutes, then Clint went to the police station to tell Sergio what Judi had learned.

"I found out that Sylvia has been asking a lot of questions about somebody she calls Nicky. He's supposed to be from Colombia and she says she knew him a little in Cali and Medillin. She thinks he works for drug lords – big surprise here," Sergio reported. "I think I want to know a lot about her. Maybe she's the important one, while John is just being used.

"Yeah! I believe that!"

"It looks like there're a bunch of weird people involved. There has to be something about that chest that's a lot more behind this than the treasure or the cash," Clint mused. "Can you arrange for me to give it a close going-over?"

"I'll be with you and say I've hired you. We did that before. It's locked in the big vault."

They went over to the property department and through to a room that was triple-walled. It had the most valuable things, confiscated or otherwise, there. The chest was in its own area, the cash neatly stacked beside it with the count and the ID's of the people who counted it. The slip said there was one million four hundred eighty eight thousand two hundred dollars.

"Who stole the twelve grand?" Clint asked. Sergio laughed and said that was the least anyone had taken from such a find yet. It was taken before it got to the property room. Clint noted that he and Sergio had to have positive ID to enter the room. Their pictures were taken along with a fingerprint scan. Sergio was the jefe of the police and had to furnish the same things a stranger would. Good system.

There was a careful listing of the other contents, which were replaced into the chest. Clint mostly ignored that and the money, except for the twenty money bands that had the initials on them. He carefully checked every inch of the chest itself, finding nothing new.

He sat back to think, then shrugged.

"Sergio, I think whatever was here was taken ... or maybe not!" Clint exclaimed. He thought a moment, then asked, "Why were only those twenty bands marked? Could there be a reason?"

Sergio grinned and said they would find out. They slipped the bills out of the bands. There was nothing on the inside of the bands.

Clint inspected the bills themselves and soon exclaimed, "Clever! Sergio, note that there are bills with a single letter in the left margin near the bottom. Six of them in this stack. Take them in order and they read, 'e-l-e-v-e-n' See if it holds."

Sergio picked up a stack and said, "I've got 's-i-x-t-e-e-n' in this one. 't-h-r-e-e-n-i-n-e' in this."

They went into all of them, listed the letters, then carefully slipped them back into the bands in the same order they were found.

"We have a neat puzzle," Clint then said. "We have the numbers and the a name, Southern.

"The number are an account. Southern is a clue to which bank it's in."

"Southern ... Trust?" Sergio wondered. "There used to be a Southern Something Trust. Offshore. It merged with Secure Sentry Bank about thirty years ago. We come across it, at times.

"Now! How do we find the proper order for the numbers?"

"It'll be something ... crap! We don't have the order of the packages in the chest."

"It won't be that. They were loose enough that they could change positions a bit."

"Hmmm. Then it'll be something on the top or bottom bill."

They checked, but there was nothing. Clint was inspecting a package and said, "How about the serial numbers of the top or bottom bills? This top one starts with a three. So does the bottom."

They checked. That was true of all the money pack-ages. Top and bottom were the same.

They ended up with 43971652902001103642.

"It's a matter of hyphens. We have the bank and number we can check," Sergio suggested. "Clint, what if there's been a few tens of millions of dollars deposited and sitting for fifty years? With the interest, what would it be now?"

"Sheeez!" was his only reply.

They went back out and were searched. Even the chief!

In Sergio's office, they contacted Secure Sentry, who said there was no way to find out anything about accounts there, so piss off. Not in those words. Sergio said there was a dead person who had an account there for fifty years, since before the merger with Southern. The heir could cause them a lot of grief. He'd give the turkey on the phone half an hour and call back. All he wanted was information for the heir. They *did* have the account number.

"In what name?" he asked.

"It should be in the .. Blakley."

"Those numbers do not match any account in the name of Blakley. It is not here."

"Then it will be Halverson or the company name," Clint replied.

"I can tell you there is something from nineteen sixty one in the name of Halverson ... WOOO! Seventy million dollars original deposit, now one hundred fifty six million dollars! You're very damned lucky that was before we had to worry about drug money laundering!"

"That makes a difference, now?" Clint couldn't stop himself from asking.

He laughed. "Now we have to account for where particularly large sums come from – large being over ten million dollars. If you can produce a receipt for selling land for the ten mil, it isn't seriously questioned, later, if you ever need the information. I think it is not our responsibility to authenticate such receipts if they are presented in a legal form, which means with a notary seal.

"Colombians, Mexicans and Peruvians seem to sell a *lot* of land at *very* high prices. Certain gringos, too. Did you know a small villa in Ft. Lauderdale sold for more than fifty million dollars? In the middle of the land crash?"

They laughed a bit. Clint promised he'd tell the heir what she had inherited so she could make a claim.

"Well, that accounts for a lot of things," Clint said, when he hung up. "What in the hell will Gina do with a hundred fifty million?"

"She can give whatever of it she has no use for to me!" Sergio suggested – which got him a middle finger salute.

Next step; find out how the other players fit in. That was Brandon and wife or whatever. They were another weird part of this. Clint still had a nagging feeling that something was a long way off-center. How would Avenidas and/or whoever else know about the bank numbers being in that chest?

They didn't. It was another thing that happened to come up in an unexpected manner and at an unexpected time. Clint checked all his recent correspondence, then went back into town to Avenidas' office to tell Gina that she may have a hundred fifty million dollars soon, but she wasn't to let it get to her to where she'd lead a life of hedonistic depravity. She laughed and said she liked the lifestyle. Did she really have to change?

"I'm serious, you know," Clint said. "You'll probably get a good bit of that. You'll have to pay capital gains taxes on about thirty million, which isn't too bad, here. It will leave you enough to live on."

She treated it as a joke. He couldn't convince her he was serious.

Avenidas came in and asked what the joke was. She said she inherited a hundred million or so. She thought that was a fun idea.

"A hundred fifty million. Plus," Clint corrected. "It's in a bank account her father had. Offshore. The part in the chest was just an emergency fund that was never used."

Avenidas looked back and forth between them, then said, "You can't be serious. That treasure chest? What does that have to do with anything?"

"The bank account number and the registration details were in the chest with the money. Sergio and I found it and checked it out. It's there. Blakley was killed for nothing."

"How would that get in an old chest?" he demanded. "Oh! The money. Then. Damn! It was right there like a lost ... I mean, that's turning out to be *some* treasure chest!"

"Clint! You're not ... serious! You *can't* be serious!" Gina cried. "Are you saying Betina Blakley was killed for that ... what was in the chest? How would she be, I mean, I don't know what I mean."

"Well, her, but I meant her father. She killed him to get the money. She thought the papers he stole from your father – you, actually – left it to him, so she could get it. Your father was smarter than that. It was all in his name, so it's all yours, now."

"I knew he had to have left something for me, but ... my god!"

"Well, it's about settled, in a way. Do you know John Brandon?"

"I knew a John Brandon in Houston when I went to school. He was a friend of my father. Father was teaching him some kind of import business or something. He's about forty five now, I'd guess."

"Brandon? There is a Somebody Brandon here who was asking a lot of questions about me a couple of months ago. Sara, the girl at the café across the street, told me about him," Avenidas said. "He was interested in stocks, but he never came here."

"He was watching you for several years," Clint said. "He and his wife tried to drug me, for some reason I can't figure."

Avenidas was looking somewhere between terrified and mad as hell. Maybe both. Gina was just confused.

"Well, I'm going home to clean up. Want to try the food at The Rip Tide? It's supposed to be as good as anywhere here. I haven't tried it, yet."

"Are you trying to pick me up just because I'm now filthy rich?" Gina demanded. "I still don't believe a word of this crap, you know, but it is kind of fun to think what it would be like if it was real."

"Well, that's not the *only* reason," Clint fired back. "I heard you're as wild as you look like you'd be."

"Oh? Who's telling you beddie-bye stories? Ben?"

"He's wild, too, if you can believe the gossip." Clint wasn't about to be one-upped like this.

"I can tell you – he *is*!" she fired back.

So she got him. He gave her the middle finger. She laughed and said she'd like to try the place. Everywhere he'd taken her, so far, has been exceptional.

He went out with Avenidas right behind. He said to have a cup of coffee with him. Clint knew he wanted to pump him for information, so he agreed. He'd get exactly the information Clint wanted to feed him. Clint soon saw Avenidas was curious about all the wrong things. He wasn't as clever as he thought he was. He wouldn't lead Clint to telling him things he really wanted to know. The old backdoor psychology ploy only worked when the subject hadn't read the book. He did learn that Avenidas knew more about Brandon than he was letting on. It wouldn't be a good idea to seem interested enough to ask any questions about him. Yet.

The food at The Rip Tide was as good as reputed. It was different than most of the food in Bocas. Clint and Gina had a very good time. They meant to go to a couple of places, but the crowd there was right for them, and friendly. Dave wandered in about ten with his guitar and played a few numbers from the seventies and earlier. *Leaving On A Jet Plane, 500 Miles*, then some heavier Janis Joplin stuff, then a little Eagles and CCR, then left about a quarter to eleven. About eleven, Gina said she had to get her beauty rest, so would head for the hotel. Clint said his place was as close and more comfortable. She thought about it, then they went to his place.

In the morning, Clint took Gina to the Bahia. Her room had been searched by someone who wanted her to know it had been searched. Things were moved and left open. She said searching her stuff was a waste of time if there ever was one, but they could have at least straightened things up better. Magali, the girl doing the maid bit in the rooms, gave Clint a look. He told Gina he'd wait outside for her to get changed, then he'd walk her to the office.

Magali told Clint that some thuggy-looking guy had been hanging around. She was sure he'd been in some of the rooms, Gina's among them. Clint nodded and gave her a five. Gina came out and they walked to the office. Avenidas wasn't there, again.

Clint went back to the Bahia. He'd seen a guy by the ferry dock that looked thuggy, to Clint. He had seen him several times. He always noted people in places who didn't quite fit. He went inside and had Magali come out to look him over. He was the one who was hanging around.

Nick walked toward him. He noticed and started to walk the other way, but Clint caught up to him.

"I'm Clint Faraday, as you undoubtably know. Who are you? Who do you work for?

"I'll tell you damned flatly that messing with Gina is going to get you turned into fish bait."

"No habla Inglés!" he cried.

"Like hell you don't! You were talking to Bob, at the Golden Grill. He doesn't speak Spanish. You were talking to Norman Flannery at The Toro Loco. He doesn't speak more than five words of Spanish. You're playing a dangerous game, hijo de puta!"

He looked at Clint and bunched his shoulders. Clint waited until he took his swing, stepped inside, and flattened him with a hard right to the solar plexus. He was on the pavement, gasping and clutching at his chest, as several people came running up. Clint said his friend wasn't watching where he was walking and had tripped over a pothole. Wasn't that what happened?

The thug nodded. A woman grinned at him and gave him a thumb up. Jorge, a police officer Clint knew, came over. He had been on the dock and had seen the whole thing. He winked at Clint.

"Sir, you must be more careful," he said. "Some of the streets here are in poor repair. Should I take you to hospital? I can carry you in the truck."

The thug shook his head.

"Well, let me take your identification so I may file a report."

The thug stood up shakily and said there was no need to file a report. He wouldn't be so careless, in the future.

"You are not from Panamá," Jorge replied, formally. "Please present your passaporte or other identification whenever asked by any police official or you will be detained for investigation."

The thug passed him his passport. Jorge said, "Nicolo Franko Bendetti of Houston, Texas. It is in order. You may go." He turned away.

"So. How are things, Nicky?" Clint asked. "You used the name of Frank in Houston with the late Betina, I believe?

"Very interesting. Who got you here? Why?"

"I ain't got nothing to do with nothing here!" he spat. "The one who brought me here is dead!"

"You were described as a wannabe thug," Clint replied, easily. "You didn't pass the test. Go back home. You won't last another week here."

"I ain't got enough to get back. She never paid me nothing yet. I was only here so I could be a sort of bodyguard. I only got here day before yesterday. I was only looking for the cash to get home in the hotel rooms."

"How much will it cost for you to get back?" Clint asked.

"I got maybe forty bucks. It cost a hunnert and fifteen for the bus and I got to eat."

Clint gave him a hundred dollars and told him to be gone within the hour.

So! Why did Betina think she needed a bodyguard? One that showed up a few hours after she was killed?

Clint went back to see if Sergio knew anything more. Very little. He called Manny. Nothing new. He called Manolo, who said the skinny was that somebody in Colombia was very interested, but probably because they could be connected, if the wrong things happened. He had promised that, if they weren't involved and if it wasn't recent, it would go away. Clint agreed to go along with that.

How come everything that happened tended to make less sense out of it? Why couldn't he make any of it come together in ... he wasn't going to start that again! He needed some place where this would start to make sense. He had it pretty much together until Avenidas and Blakley came to Bocas. The only way it figured was that neither of them knew about the cash in the chest. They damned well didn't know about the codes on the bills. That was where they got off whatever tracks they were on. That's where it became necessary to get rid of Betina. Why? Because the money was now totally out of their reach? Then why kill Betina? She expected trouble, is why Nicky-boy was sent for. The trouble came eight or ten hours before he arrived.

Avenidas had been promised something, the same as Bendetti had. She was in a position where she could have ... what?

Sergio said it was very obviously a rage killing. That could well be. Avenidas had been promised whatever could get him out of trouble with those drug cartels. She wasn't going to deliver. It could have been rage over that – but Clint saw fear. Terror. When Avenidas was faced with the fact she was dead, he had gone into an act that was just a bit too much to believe, but that terror was in his eyes and body language. Very clearly.

It could be figured and closed, except for one thing. John and Sylvia tried to drug him to find out something. That had to mean they thought he knew something he didn't know. That meant that Gina knew whatever it was.

Did she know something she wasn't aware of? Did it mean she knew something she *was* aware of?

Clint liked more action and less thinking. The thinking part was supposed to lead to the action, but all it was doing was leading to more thinking. He decided to put a little pressure on Avenidas. He could hope that would lead him to learning what Brandon's part was, in this mess. That was what made no sense in any scenario he could picture.

He saw Judi going into the gourmet, so went in to ask if she'd learned anything that might give him something.

"Not much. Sylvia Gordas seems to have some kind of connection with drug cartels or whatever. She knows all the wrong people."

"I take it Gordas is her real name. Those drug cartels are coming up much too often in this. I worry about them getting any of their shit started here.

"I think Manny can find something, if they're part of it. We can give him a name to work back from.

"I think I'll open a PI agency here. You and Manny do as much as I do in this."

"It passes the time." She grinned. "You still don't have a definite direction to finding what this was about, do you?"

"Oh, I have several. Only problem is connecting more than two together. Get the third in any angle and the other two don't fit, anymore."

They went to the Starfish and had a cup of hugely overpriced coffee, then Clint went back home, while Judi went to Almirante and Changuinola with some friends to shop. It's cheaper to buy almost anything there than in Bocas, so a trip a week for groceries and household needs saved more than enough to pay for the water taxi and bus. A call to Manny got it started as to who and what Sylvia Gordas was and what her part of it might be. That should tie John Brandon in, one way or another. He hoped.

Next was a little run out toward Drago. He saw a boat on the beach just past The Bluffs and two people, a man and a woman, using a metal detector. People would scour every single inch of the beach area since the find. Several Indios were watching to see they didn't go onto the private land above the tide line.

No one would bury anything below the tide line. Couldn't they see that?

A couple of the Indios saw Clint and waved to him. He waved back and did the circle to the side of the head with his finger. It said, "Loco." They agreed, and laughed. One of them waved a twenty dollar bill at Clint. Clint put his hands up and shrugged. The Indio pointed inland a little, to a tree about fifteen feet from the tide line, then to the two with the metal detector, which got their attention enough that the man turned to see Clint there – and told Clint that they had paid him to let them go a little above the tide line with their equipment. Clint waved and headed out.

The Indio didn't own the land, he was probably just passing by. They offered him twenty five bucks for permission to go onto the land. He didn't have an argument against giving them his permission. He didn't care. The owner of the property might come at any time to tell them to get out. No one lied to them or claimed the right to give permission. What they assumed was their problem.

On the other hand, the owner probably didn't care. The Indios wouldn't pass through his land, if he did. At least, not these particular Indios.

Clint went on to Drago and started back about an hour later. The people had managed to move about a kilometer on along the beach.

Clint shook his head. If the spot the chest had been found was any indication, he would know any other would be in a hidden recess or somewhere not in direct view of the Caribbean.

He got back and cleaned up, dressed and headed back into Bocas Town. Dave and Selma were in the parque. He talked awhile. Dave said he could have sworn he saw John Brandon in a boat out by Carenero, on the Caribbean side. He and Selma had gone to visit friends on Bastimentos. They had seen him when they were coming back. He was alone.

Curiouser and curiouser. Clint wondered if he had a metal detector with him. Dave said he didn't know him, except to say hello. He and his wife had gone to several places where Dave was playing.

Those people earlier didn't mean anything. If Brandon was out treasure-hunting, it might mean there was another chest somewhere close. That would mean ... the shocked reactions of people about the one found was because something was *not* in that chest, not because something extra was.

What? They weren't very excited by the money. What could be in a chest somewhere out there?

Clint suddenly wanted to get to the far side of Carenero to see if Brandon went to a specific spot. He grabbed a taxi and got to his boat to go out fast. He went around the northwest end of Carenero and headed along the outer side, fast. He wouldn't appear to be looking for anything that way. Just a fisherman heading in.

There were three boats along the beach there. One was at the mouth of a runnel that went onto the island. The water would be too shallow to take a boat in there, so whoever was in that boat had gone onto the island. The runnel also formed a little indent that would leave what whoever was doing there out of view. It was much like the one where the chest was found on Isla Colón. Too much.

It was getting weirder! Clint hadn't thought that would be possible. He called Sergio and said to get a boatload of police out there. Bring the metal detectors he had and get the one at his place.

"What have you discovered?" he asked.

"I wish to *hell* I knew!" Clint said, as the saying goes, "With great emotion."

Clint watched as Brandon moved along the inner side of the curve of the runnel with a metal detector. He was slogging around in the loose mud. Chitras were eating him alive, if he didn't have a hell of a lot of Deet. They were always bad on Carenero. Sergio and the police came up and were talking with Clint when Brandon saw them. He casually went to his boat and slid the metal detector in, then pushed it off the beach and started out. Sergio was going to stop him, but Clint said to ignore him for the moment. He wasn't going far.

Basilio, an Indio friend on the police force, said the idiot didn't know much about the area if he was searching the runnel for something that was buried fifty years ago. The runnel wasn't there that long. "The runnels bring out mud and trees and everything else after a storm and fill in as they move along. You can see there are no old trees around here. If you notice the kinds of trees, you can see where the old runnel was. Fifty years ago ... about thirty years ago the runnel filled in so much it moved. You have to find where the trees are all less than thirty years old to know where it was. The hardwoods. The regular trees grow fast enough that you couldn't tell. I would say it was about fifty meters northward ... just a minute." He walked along the beach and said it could be there, but he thought it was about fifteen meters farther along. The runnel had moved twice. It might be either spot. The last one could be a very old run.

"You can tell where the shores were. There are older hardwoods to the edge. See those with the small leaves? They have been there for several hundred years. No less than one hundred. Move along just outside of them ...

no, just inside of them. The box would have been buried by the shore, not in the runnel. We have to check both places."

Clint didn't doubt the information would be one hundred percent accurate.

They didn't find anything there before it started getting dark. Sergio left two officers in one of the boats to sit out a bit to observe if anyone came. He would send two others out to relieve them at the end of their shift.

"Just observe and note time and exact locations they go to. Don't interfere or try to approach them. We have to know more before we do the wrong thing," Clint suggested. They agreed. They would come back at daybreak to continue their search. Clint went in to his house, cleaned up, and dressed again, then went in to meet Gina to go to The Plank, where Dave would be playing. Not much else happened. It was a good evening. Selma had gone with Judi to see Almirante and Changuinola, so Clint, Ben, Manny (who had come in to take care of some business) and two Indio friends finished the night, after Gina went back to the hotel. She wanted to be alone awhile to figure out what she was going to do now. She still wasn't altogether convinced she was going to get any thousands of dollars, much less millions.

Clint went home. Dave went home. Ben went home – with the Indios.

"I'll take the older runnel, with Ronaldo and David. You take the newer one, with Sandoval and Pablito," Sergio instructed. "Move along where you can cover about five meters from where the shore was. Go up the north side and return along the south."

They all agreed and started the search. It would be slow progress. They had machetes to chop their way through the lighter brush. Just after one o'clock, Ronaldo called that he had found a large piece of metal. Sergio called to keep looking, in case it wasn't what they were after. He used a probe and started to dig down to the object. It was about three feet deep. The covering soil was a little rocky and hard to dig, but there were no large stones. Just as he called that it did seem to be some kind of metal box, Pablito found something, so they would probe and dig, if it seemed likely. It was also a metal box. By the time they had reached it, Sergio had the whole top of his box uncovered. He said it would take them all to lift it out of there, so they went to take some poles they cut to use as levers and got it to the surface. It had a large padlock that had rusted almost off holding the lid closed, through brass hasps. All the hinges and bands were brass. The box was wood covered in copper, inside and out. The wood had rotted away.

Sergio said they would have to take it back to Bocas before it was opened. He wouldn't take responsibility for it, here. They agreed, and put it in one of the boats, then went together to dig up the other. It was much like the first, but appeared to be much newer. It didn't have such fancy brasswork. It was basically steel. It was more like a copy of an old treasure chest for the movies, or something.

"You know what?" Clint asked.

"I would suggest that we found an actual pirate treasure – and what we were looking for. Both," Sergio answered.

"This is even weirder than I thought," Clint agreed.

They took their loot back to Bocas Town to put it in the secure vault before they opened it. The entire crew who dug it up were there. They had the right.

The treasure chest, the authentic one, had some very good jewelry and a lot of gold in it. There were almost a hundred pounds of gold coins, alone. They very carefully listed every piece. Clint put a handfull of the more common coins in a bucket and held the bucket at eye level, then told each one in the crew to reach in and take one coin. Sergio started to protest, but Clint said this was less than usual and these people deserved a souvenir. He would expect Sergio to see that they got them out of the vault. Sergio laughed. He said he was going to take one, himself, in that case.

They remade one list with the coins selected omitted.

They turned to the other chest. It was the one that interested them, is why they left it for last. It was stacked full of money. Nothing else. No codes or anything. Hundred dollar bills, all more than fifty years old.

Clint sat back to think while the men counted the stacks.

"Sergio, they used a code on the others. I think this was the real object – but why? Why not write it off? If they got by without it for fifty years, why come for it in a panic now?"

"I would say, because the existence of this much money buried at that time told a story we haven't been able to read. Yet."

"That doesn't work. There would be no way to connect this to anything, after all that time. There has to be something that would point directly to someone or something. Something deadly to someone. Someone big enough that he didn't come after however much is in there a long time ago."

"How much is here?" Serge asked Ronaldo.

"We have listed less than an eighth of it. It is more than twelve (Clint said he *hated* that damned number) million dollars. The stacks are 114 deep by ten long by twenty six wide. That comes to twenty nine thousand six hundred twenty packages. There is five thousand dollars in each package. That is one hundred forty eight million two hundred thousand dollars."

"With no way to know who put it there, so we still don't have a reason for any of this."

"There's a code in there, somewhere, that tells us exactly who. Are you sure there's nothing on those bills?" Clint asked.

"Nothing," Sergio said. "Other than the fact so many of them are in series and can ... Clint! This is marked money! Those serial numbers will tell us who!"

Clint grabbed his phone and called Manolo to ask if they had the serial numbers of hundred dollar bills from fifty years ago that were used in a deal and have never shown up.

There was a dead silence for a full minute, then, "Have you found the Juan Toren money? More than one hundred forty five million have never been found or used. That's fifty one years ago next week."

"We found a hundred forty eight million of it. Why is it so important that they'd go to the extremes they have over it?"

"It'll prove which major cartel family was in on selling out four others. If that's found, there'll then be no one to the second cousin in that family alive within three days. Three of the four families sold out have, as we say, recovered their fortunes and power. The fourth earned enough to retire in comfort."

"Shit!" Clint cried, making Sergio and the others jump. "Thanks, Manolo. You can arrange for someone to claim the money, if it matches the serial numbers – and it will. How much will I get for finding it?”

“Demand ten percent. You’ll get it.”

“It’ll be for a school and hospital somewhere in the area,” Clint promised. “We also found a legitimate pirate treasure.”

“No shit? The other one wasn’t?”

“The pirate treasure part was. This isn’t quite as good quality, but it’s still good – Oh! Maybe you can find who John Brandon works for. That’ll be the family that won’t be here in a few days.”

Manolo agreed to try. They talked a minute, then hung up.

“Clint, be careful. Those people might go wild, here, and try to kill off everyone who even knows there was a treasure found.”

“I intend to be very careful. I intend to protect my friends and the innocent.”

They took about another half hour of counting before Clint left to go find Gina at the office. Avenidas was there. Clint told about finding the treasure and the second box. He said they were trying to trace the money, that there was nothing there *but* the money. The US treasury was checking to see if they had any records. The bills were in series, so might be marked money.

Avenidas was about to die of heart failure, by the look of him. “Er, how much was there?” he asked.

“We’d estimate around a hundred fifty million.”

He squealed and went back to his office. Clint said he was going home to clean up. He’d come back when it was time for her to leave. It might not be a good idea for her to be alone much until something about this was settled, though he was sure her part wasn’t in the danger zone, as he called it. It was the box they found today that was where the danger remained. At least a good part of it was explained. It also explained why there was so little connection to anything before.

He met Selma and Judi on the way home. They had come back from Changuinola about an hour before. He caught them up. Selma said that kind of money was just plain obscene. She knew one person in Florida who had that kind of money and more who was a decent, worthwhile human being. She knew ten who were pains in the ass and about as worthless as anyone could be.

Clint saw his place had been searched, very professionally. His little traps made that plain, but whoever it was found his cameras and erased the computer records. There wasn't anything there to find. Clint had been around enough to where he knew what not to leave around. Nothing was bothered, much.

He relaxed a bit, then went to walk with Gina to the Bahia. She wouldn't stay at his place. That may be dangerous to them both, in her mind. If someone thought she knew anything that was as serious as Clint said, killing them both would be much more likely. She wouldn't be alone at anytime, except in her room – and she would manage to move to another without anyone knowing.

Avenidas had left, early. He looked like death warmed over, as she put it. Sergio called to say that an officer had seen Brandon in town and was discretely keeping an eye on him to see who he met.

Clint went back home. He could use a long night to just sleep, now and then. Either things were going to get more tranquil, fast – or all hell was going to break loose, faster.

"Clint? Someone was watching your place from a boat since before dawn. What's that about?" Judi greeted him, in the morning.

"What kind of boat?"

"A sixteen or eighteen foot Wellcraft. White with green trim."

"Brandon? Why would he be watching me? This shit isn't going to get weird again, I hope. Thanks, Judi."

He went out on the deck with binoculars and made it a point to let Brandon know he was being observed. Brandon waved and came toward the dock. Clint waited until he was right beside the deck to ask what he wanted. He said he had to know what was in that chest. It was important in ways he couldn't guess.

"After you drugged me for the information and didn't get any, you would just come here and ask me?" Clint said. "You're weird, man."

"I figured you might talk without the added aggravation. The scope was *not* my idea."

"Okay. Who's going to end up with no heirs, and planted, himself over this?" Clint replied.

"So you found the significance of the thing. I was worried about that. Sylvia is in it up to her neck. I'm not. I wish I'd never met her. She's a Cano."

Clint nodded in a knowing way to disguise the fact he didn't have a clue as to who the Canos were.

"I suppose the states will have traced the serial numbers, by now," he said. "That's all I can see that would tell anyone about that money. There was nothing else in the chest. Most of the money was in series in the original bank bands.

"Is Sylvia Darlin' a Cano – within second cousin?"

"No, but her half brother is. A nephew."

Clint nodded, again. "Does he know anything that certain agencies might find interesting?"

"To hear them brag, you'd think so. I'm not at all convinced any of them stick within spitting distance of the truth. He might."

"Then he has a very slight chance, if he can get to one of those agencies before the aggressive parties get to him. They'll make a good deal for protection."

"There isn't any way to perhaps delay ... I guess not, if you've sent the serial numbers out. You know a lot more than they guessed about it.

"Does the Halverson woman know anything, or is she just caught up in the intrigues because of who her father was?"

"The latter."

"I can at least make that clear. I can't make any guarantees. None of them have a chance, anyhow. No telling what they'll do."

"As you say, they don't have a chance, anyhow, so what good would it do to go after her?"

He shook his head. "You don't know how those people, excuse the expression, think," he said, with a grimace. "Thanks. I wish you hadn't found that chest. The word is that you found two. What's that about?"

"One was an authentic treasure chest."

"Christ! Why couldn't I have found that?!"

"Because you didn't know where to look."

"I noticed you went away from the runnel. I didn't hang around out there. How did you find it?"

"We asked an Indio where to look. He said the runnel wasn't where it is now, fifty years ago. We found an even older runnel path and checked out both. Both had chests."

"The Indios know that much about where to look?! Why didn't they?!"

"They aren't interested in old treasures. They bring more trouble than they're worth," Clint said. "You haven't a clue as to how they think. They tend to be practical and basic. Treasure may be pretty or whatever, but you can't eat it, it won't keep you warm or cool, it doesn't cure sickness. Leave it to when you have the time to waste on such things."

"But they can sell the stuff and have everything!"

"The government gets most of it and will screw them out of the rest."

"But ... why? I mean ... Christ!"

"Their culture doesn't have ownership, as any real part of it. I can't explain it. You don't even have the basic concepts."

He shook his head. "I guess so. Thanks. I appreciate your help. I wish we had simply asked you about things before. You would probably have told us."

Clint nodded. "Most of it, anyway."

Brandon headed out. Clint went back inside and called Manolo. "Cano," is all he said.

There was a short silence. "It positive or an educated guess?"

"The half-brother of Sylvia Gordas is a Cano. Nephew. He's afraid he won't survive the day."

"Tell him to contact Peter P. Hanson. He can possibly be protected and put on a witness protection plan in the states. They *really* want information about Josefus Cano and his cronies!"

"Within three days, there won't *be* any Canos," Clint pointed out. "Problem finally brought to a reasonable conclusion."

"But we can get very valuable information from them, if we can get to them before the others do."

"There is that," Clint agreed.

He chatted awhile more, then called Manny to tell him what he'd learned. Manny said he sort of thought it might be Cano. He was very cool about it and the operative, then said he was the only one who wasn't scared shitless among them all. Now the family will be wiped out because of what grandpa did. Grandpa – who died thirty five years ago.

"I sort of feel sorry for some of them. They got trapped into something before they were born. Something they didn't have a clue about."

"I think the ones who got out of the business will be Okay. The ones still in it don't get any sympathy from me!"

"I suppose," Clint replied. "How's the wife and family?"

"Point taken. I don't have anything like that hanging over me. I wonder if maybe Pop did, but I'm sure he would have warned me."

They talked a little more. Manny would come into Bocas about seven. They would get a meal and spend some time getting to know Gina, who Judi had said would probably end up a permanent part of their group. Everyone liked her – and she was seriously considering being a more or less permanent part of Clint's life.

Clint learned the strangest things about his own life this way!

"Avenidas seems to have skipped – or would have. The idiot union has all the taxi boats blocked from coming and going, here," Dave announced. He was with Gina at the new little restaurant where four or five had already failed near the office. "He's either paid somebody to take him to Almirante or he's hiding somewhere here on the island."

"What's it about?" Clint asked. "I know there were some people killed when a water taxi hit a cayuca full of people, then the water taxis are blocked. Everybody knows that was the fault of the driver of the water taxi, no one else. How did any union get into that mess?"

"They're using it for an excuse. It's like the big union crap in the states, awhile back. They did this kind of thing, as much as the government let them get by with, got their union, thought they were getting a better deal and would make a lot of money, paid union fees. That bunch of crime syndicate got rich, wages went up about ten percent, then prices went up twenty percent, they were paying union dues, on top of it. They actually lost their asses and those crooked unions are still there and still a major base of inflation. Credit got easy, so everybody seemed to have more than ever, but they were in debt up to their eyeballs, until the credit crash came along – but they could get money from their credit union and go into debt even more ... why am I preaching to the choir?" Dave said, disgustedly. "The same thing will happen here. It's part of the human stupidity condition. It's all there to see, but history has never been listened to and never will. People are collectively stupid. It could turn your stomach.

"Off the soapbox. Would Manny know when and how many Canos are getting erased?"

"He'll be here, later. So long as none of the innocent are involved, I say to let it lie," Clint said.

"What about the relatives who aren't involved in it?" Gina asked. "No one gives a thought to them."

"Manny says things have changed enough that anyone who got out of the crap that started it will probably be alright. They don't go after anyone not still in the business," Judi said. "I think I agree with Manny about that. If you stayed in the business, I can't work up any sympathy for you."

They changed the subject, for awhile, but got back to it. They knew things would be hard to get until the water taxis and ferry were running again. The people who would actually be hurt were the tourists and businesses that catered to them. Then the very people who were on strike would suffer. Groceries and supplies would become a problem. The people who lived out of Bocas Town wouldn't have much trouble, except at the tourist hotels. Tourism would be hurt, very badly, for a couple of years more, minimum. Maybe permanently, because prices on the island would skyrocket. It was going to cost a lot more to get anything out there. It was already known that prices on Isla Colón were at least double those as close as Almirante, on the mainland. That was why Judi and her friends went to Almirante and Changuinola every month. If it was going to cost more on the taxis, they would pool and use someone's boat among their own small group. Screw the idiocy. Martinelli was a businessman. He could surely see what was going to happen to tourism because of this.

"What do you suggest?" Gina asked.

"Well, they're blocking public access on the water, which is public property. Round up the union thugs and put them away for a couple of years," Dave suggested.

"How could he ever get away with that?!" Judi asked.

"Reagan got away with it in the states. The general public, who he's supposed to protect, was being hurt. Business was being hurt. The economy was being hurt. The airlines, themselves, weren't the important feature. They were a necessity," Dave said, drily. "That water traffic is necessary to the economy of Panamá. DO something about it!

"I thought we were going to talk about something else."

"There's nothing but that and the Cano thing to talk about," Judi pointed out. Dave gave her the finger.

They decided to wander around a bit. Avenidas figured that he was safer with them than alone, in hiding, and found them. They didn't want him around, but he would drag along. Dave asked him if he was a Cano or just involved for some other reason.

"I'm a second cousin," he said.

"You aren't in any danger unless you're still involved with them," Judi said.

He didn't answer that. Clint smirked at him and said, eventually, what you do comes back to haunt you. As the Seger song says, no one gets to walk between the rain.

"But you can carry an umbrella," Gina said. "Oh! WE'RE your umbrella."

"If the wind whips up too strong, an umbrella becomes a liability," Dave replied. "What are we doing now? Competing for the worst metaphor of the month?" Everyone except Avenidas gave him the finger.

"Mr. Faraday, it is well-known that you are acquainted with some powerful people involved in that business.

Could I impose upon you to have them intercede? I am *not* involved in that kind of thing. I'm merely stretching the rules a bit in the real estate and stockbroker business. No one is hurt who can't afford it."

"Then why was Betina Blakley here?" Clint asked. "We aren't that stupid. There ain't no way any of my friends – who are in the Mediterranean at the moment – will get involved in this kind of thing."

"I knew there was a very large cache of money hidden somewhere in the area. I thought it may be as much as two million dollars. Those things are always exaggerated. I also knew she would be the only person in the world who would know how to find it. The fact that her father paid me for certain services with articles from the chest told me that.

"She's the one who killed her own father, you know. I have no sympathy with what happened to her."

"*You* happened to her," Clint said. "As you might say, she deserved worse. I don't really care about her. I care about what's happened since."

"When that chest was found, it was a shock to me that there was so much money. I think she was the one who caused its discovery. She didn't know much about it. She did know there was some money in the chest, I think. She would claim she had rights to the contents, except for the money. When it was found to contain millions, she panicked. That would mean explanations she couldn't tender, if she knew about the chest in the first place.

"Then Jul ... a certain person contacted her and me. Very powerful people in Colombia wanted to know what was in the chest. Relatives of mine.

"I did not kill her – but I was there. She didn't know where the second chest was. The man from the family became enraged. He killed her when she said he could kiss her ass. She wouldn't be intimidated enough to tell trash such as he anything. No man would ever again make her do anything.

"His sister, therefore a more distant relative of mine, is living with a man, here, for the purpose of observing. That second chest must not be discovered, then it was. John Brandon took it upon himself to find the chest. He had no idea of what it contained or why it was so important. He was drawn into it through his naivete. You observed him and found the chest. When it was reported that you found absolutely nothing in that chest to point to anyone, everybody relaxed. Then you checked the serial numbers of those bills and they told the whole story. It was marked money. It was plain from that point who had received the money, thus who was the person who sold out competing businessmen to the E.U.A. Only they would have a hundred fifty million dollars cash with registered serial numbers as to who received the money. They never stop looking for such sums. None of it ever was passed.

"You know the rest – or the parts that could concern anyone here, except for myself and any other close relative of Josefus Cano."

"Yes. Sylvia's half-brother," Clint said.

"Half-brother?" he snarled. "She doesn't have any *half*-brother. She had two brothers. She's a niece. She hasn't hidden that from them with a bunch of phony papers. They know one hell of a lot more about how that works than she does!"

"Apparently, she thinks she's safe," Clint said.

"No one is safe. She's involved in the wrong parts of it," Avenidas replied. "I worry that John, who is a rather decent sort, might end up dead because of this. He doesn't have any way to know about what's involved.

He doesn't know anything about the relatives or the money or anything else the rest of the people here know.

"There is the blessing that it is so difficult to reach the island right now, but it is also most difficult to leave."

"Brandon has a boat. She can leave," Dave said. "You can come and go, it's just more expensive now.

"Apparently, Julio is still here. Did you consider that?"

"Who ... Okay. I made that slip. Julio is family. He's also marked for extinction. He's Sylvia's brother. We might arrange to use the Brandon boat, but that will be watched. We would be going right to them, no matter where we went."

"How much information do you have?" Clint asked.

"A lot. I learned a great deal from my father and uncle and have kept abreast of the situations and persons since I was fifteen years old."

"Take the boat to ... like you're on your way to Cusapin. It would be logical that you might hide there for quite a time. Get a throwaway cell phone, leave me the number. No one else. I'll arrange for a person to contact you when you're in a certain area on the way. If anyone can make you disappear, he can. You will answer any calls to that phone with the words, 'It's your dime. Habla.' The answer will be, 'Bloody hell! I got the wrong number!' It'll probably cost you. He's not in the charity business. He'll make a deal with people from here and the US who need your information. I'll tell you flatly that he'll also sell them the information. He will not sell to the highest bidder. He has that going for him. Within his ... area of expertise, he is known as being completely trustworthy.

"It's your only chance. I think he can protect you until the people who want the information can take over. There's a good chance they can protect you."

"We have no choice. To refuse is suicide."

Manny came up. Clint explained that Avenidas wanted to make a deal with a mutual friend who was in the Mediterranean – and who would not make deals for this kind of thing. He explained what he was setting up. Manny, who was the person who was supposed to be in the Mediterranean, nodded. He said maybe it would work. He couldn't think of a better plan.

Avenidas called Sylvia, who said their place was being watched. They didn't dare go outside, though they might be a little safer because it was so hard to leave. It was an island, so the police could find them pretty fast.

"Get the boat, get the two others, meet me at the ferry dock. Don't take much, but bring all the cash you can get together. All of you. We have one chance. I'll tell you about it on the boat. Be sure there is all the fuel we can carry.

"Sylvia. You are not to involve John in this, at all! Is that quite clear?"

He soon rang off and said she'd meet him on the dock in twenty minutes. He would gather what he could carry and the cash he had and be there. He would greatly appreciate it if the group would stay together for the twenty minutes.

He went to the internet café where Digicel had a promotion and bought a ten dollar phone and two dollars time, then to his rooming house to gather some things he had packed for when he planned to hide on the island. They got to the dock about four minutes before the Brandon boat came. Clint had noted the man watching. He had also called Sergio to have the police boat in the area. The Brandon boat would be followed. The police would stop the follower for a safety check and license check. The Brandon boat would go around like it was heading directly for Almirante, then would detour behind Sheppard's Island and behind Isla San

Cristóbal, through Dolfin Bay, and out through the Zapatillos. It would be easy to spot any watchers. Avenidas had instructions on what to do, if they were followed.

When they were on their way and the police boats had stopped two boats for ID and license checks. Clint et al headed for the new restaurant nearby that was supposed to be good. Clint called Manolo and told him what he'd told Avenidas. He had the number of the phone and was to call when they had enough time to be near Chiriqui Grande and to say, "Bloody hell! I got the wrong number!" when Avenidas answered with "It's your dime. Habla." That would identify him. It was up to him, after that point. Charge them whatever they could let go of and let them see him make a deal with the DEA and whatever, where he also got some cash for delivering them. In case there was ever any communication between them and the cartels, he was simply doing what everyone thought he was doing. His cover would be safe. Then they had a great night. Gina went home with Clint.

"We've gotten a few odd things done and a bit accomplished for the DEA and that kind of crap," Clint complained. "There shouldn't be much danger from that bunch, now. Why do I get the feeling something's been missed?"

"You got me there," Dave answered. "I can't see where anything's left out of what you set out to do.

"I'm taking Selma to David, then over to see some friends in Chitre. We'll spend a night in Santiago on the way back to David, then she wants to see Puerto Armuelles and Rio Sereno. She knows a couple of people in Boquete.

"What I'm saying is that I don't have the foggiest when I'll get back.

"What's Gina gonna do, now that Avenidas is obviously not going to be running any business?"

"She's going back to Colombia and then back here. She has some friends – well, I do – who can get her a residence visa."

"She gonna live with you?"

"We don't know. We get along well enough and she's the kind I can stay with."

He nodded, then went to pick Selma up and go to the Refugio to use their dock to have an Indio friend take them to Almirante. Clint went to the Golden Grill to talk with the locals. A private jet had landed just before noon. It wasn't Jimmy Buffet, so they didn't know who it was. Probably a big union boss.

"I wouldn't be at all surprised," Clint replied. "Nobody will note that the union boss has a private jet. That won't be enough to show what that bunch is. The only ones who get anything out of this kind of crap are the union bosses. No sense in worrying about it."

They talked a bit about Wild Bill and the treasure and such. Clint went to take Gina to the airport, then decided to go fishing the rest of the afternoon. Ben had a friend at his place who would like to go out for the afternoon, so he invited them along. They had a good time diving around the reef just inside of Solarte, then Clint let Ben and Earl out at The Reef Restaurant dock and went home. He went inside to find a large man about fifty five years of age and a younger one who looked like him sitting in his sala. He didn't show any surprise. He just told them that they should have called and he would have been back sooner.

"Mr. Faraday, I have heard much about you the past few days. I am in need of your services. I apologize for this intrusion, but didn't wish to wait in the town. My enemies will know I am here and that I am speaking with you, so you will be in some small danger from that, but I assure you, they dare not act against you in a violent way. It would introduce far more excessive violence that would be directed at them.

"I'm sorry! It is a breach of good manners I am seldom prone to commit. I am Jaime Serrano. I truly hope I have avoided being particularly noted by you, as of yet. This is my son, Renaldo.

"I will shut up and allow you to speak, another breach on my part."

Clint shrugged and said he didn't have a clue as to what he wanted to talk about.

"That is, I find, good. I will approach this by telling you some history – and what finding that treasure means. It is not what you think and I am not speaking of the money chest. I am speaking of the other two. The money was expected to be found, eventually. It was a most inconvenient find, at this time, but that is relegated to history."

"I was wondering what I missed. Would you like a beer?"

"That would be most kind of you."

"I will tell you of my family for the past five generations, then you will see how much of this came about.

"My grandfather, four times removed, was called El Tiburón. He was a slightly successful pirate in the Caribbean. He is important in that he fathered my grandfather four times removed, who was known as Fire Eyes, who you may have heard of. He was a more successful pirate. He is the one who actually enriched the family, greatly, with his ill-earned wealth.

"Fire Eyes was known locally – by which I mean in every port from southern Mexico to Brazil – as a man who garnered his fortune by the worst kind of means, but who spread his wealth to the people in the ports. His worst feature was that he was an extreme racist. He despised the Negroes and Indios a little more than he despised anyone not Spanish.

"My great great grandfather was a politician who tried to make up for his father's policies by favoring the Negroes and Indios, though his methods resulted in even more resentment. He was killed when the results of one of his policies, actually introduced to help the Indios, resulted in thousands of them being slaughtered for their land. He went to try to find a way to change what happened to what he had planned would happen. The Indios were, quite understandably, not too willing to listen to anything more from him. I know that his motives were good and that what happened horrified him. I have his writings of the time.

"My great grandfather inherited some maps and details of where booty was hidden along the coast. In seven locations, one of which was here on what is now Isla Carenero. The chest found on Isla Colón was not his. It was left by a pirate named Cutter. Cutter founded a branch of the family now known as Cano in Colombia.

"Our family has never been involved *with* the Canos. We have always been involved in halting the activities of that family. Many Canos are very good people. Most of them are not of the branch of the family that now disgraces the name.

"My grandfather and father merely used some of the treasure, converted into cash or melted down for their precious metals, to continue the family and to found and invest in businesses. I, as a result, own a number of companies in a variety of fields. I am what is called vastly wealthy because of the garnerings of my antecedents. I know where all the treasures are hidden. I have mostly left them there because I had hope the Indios would find them. Their cultural imperative of sharing would, until quite recently, have made them spread the wealth. Now government gets the whole thing and gives the finders a pittance, thus I decided to leave the loot where it is. I know of no government deserving of it.

"There are two left to find. I cannot say I have any wish that they ever are.

"I will now request that Renaldo leave us to speak of matters that it is far the better he knows nothing about."

Renaldo nodded, said he was glad to have met Clint and said he would go somewhere to meet the people. He found he liked Bocas and no one would know who he was. Clint suggested The Toro Loco to meet gringos or The Reef or The Pirate to meet a mixed crowd or La Iguana to meet the surfers. He said he preferred to meet the real people, so would go to a few local places.

He left, hailing a taxi in front of the entrance to Clint's property. Clint got himself and Jaime another Balboa, then sat to hear the rest of it.

"As you can see by the least observance, I have no need of money. I will go so far as to say that I have something better because it will not lose value and is quite easily converted into money of whatever description. It is gold. Literally metric tons of it, along with like amounts of silver, and even a good bit of platinum. I also have jewels of inestimable value.

"Be that as it may, the facts are that I am against the branch of the Cano family concerned here. I have great wealth that is quite literally beyond estimation, at this juncture. I am desirous on no publicity. I live very quietly. I wish for it to remain so.

"The Canos are in a position, because of the accidental discovery of that cache of money at the time my own chest was discovered, following the discovery of the Cano hoard with money added to it fifty years ago, to cause me publicity. I know you are not oriented toward money. You have earned much in the little time you are here. You have given almost all of it to causes I agree with fully – but my experience with the situation and politics here urge me to warn you that you must never relax vigilance in protecting what you have accomplished so that it falls not into the hands of others. That WILL happen, at your demise. I have great experience in that fact and tell you there is no way I've been able to find that will guarantee any of your good works will remain, except in name, what you have established.

"Perhaps you will find a way. You are quite inventive.

"I also know that Marko Boccini is Manny Mathews, but assure you that fact will not, because of me, go beyond those who now are aware of it. I think I would like to meet him. We think much alike. He wants to be away from his past. I wish to be away from my family's past. We both also wish to keep the material things we have. C'est la vie.

"Mr. Faraday, I wish to employ you to lessen the impact of those disgusting bits of refuse on my life. I am aware you do not care for money. I will fund whatever project you wish to fund, in hopes it will survive both of us." He stopped and looked expectant.

"I'll do what I can," Clint promised. "Call me Clint. I think I can respect you, even call you a friend."

"And I am Jaime. My friends, among whom I hope you are included, call me Jim."

They talked awhile. Clint got a lot of information he would pass on to Manolo. He made no bones about that. He said it would help to keep his name out of anything to cooperate with a certain few people.

"I will not ask if the man called Manolo is your contact. He is very clever and, with resources that told me who Mathews is, I have been unable to definitively show, one way or another."

"He has a sense of right and wrong. To try to appeal to him for personal reasons is a waste of time. He'll work on the side of the law when scum like the Canos are involved, but has his own thing about many other ... undertakings. I can say, definitely, that he will bust his ass to see innocent people don't get hurt by this crap or by the crap anyone else causes. He is, like you and me, protective of the Indigenos. I like their culture and I like most of them I know."

"The irony of that is that they are the people least in need of protection, a good percent of the time. They are quite able and practical, even if others don't understand, as you say, where they're coming from."

"It's simple," Clint answered. "It's also basic and beyond most other philosophies today. They have no ownership, in the sense we do, so money and possessions are really a foreign concept, to them. The result is the greed for accumulation isn't there. That, alone, puts them beyond the understanding of most.

"I have seen instances where one man, who was treated very badly by most others on Isla San Cristóbal, was the first to come to the aid of all of them during the innundation. They fixed up a big, solid, unused building on his finca, there, and slaughtered a cow and a pig to feed them.

"He didn't owe them the time of day, yet he feels it's his duty, as an Indigeno, to help at any time it's needed. After the crisis was over, he was still treated much the same by them. It's their way of life. They are a totally open society. They don't condemn anyone for being different. They may gossip a bit and giggle about it, but it isn't any of their business what anyone else does, particularly in sexual matters. The one rule is that you do *not*, under *any* circumstances, dare to involve children.

"They don't consider you children after twelve or thirteen years old. That's the part a lot of people don't understand – but most people don't do heavy work to help their own family, starting at seven or eight years of age.

"Okay. We understand a few of each other's ideas. I'm going into Bocas to meet Manny. Want to come along?"

"Decidedly!"

They went out front, met Ben and Judi coming back from Bocas. Clint introduced Jaime, simply as Jim. Judi said she was going to some friends' place for dinner and left. Ben would tag along with Clint and Jim. They went to Gary's Mexican restaurante, where they had some excellent food, then headed into town to meet Manny at The Pirate. Renaldo was there, so Clint introduced Ben, who said he was gorgeous. Jim had found that Ben was gay, almost immediately, and was a little curious and amused. He looked expectantly at Renaldo, who seemed a bit embarrassed, then asked Ben where he should go to meet people more their own age. Ben said there were a couple of places that were pretty good. They left. Jim shook his head and giggled.

"I thought I knew my son, but there are areas we have seldom discussed. This is, obviously, one of them. I knew not how he might react to someone like Ben."

"He's rather a good person, isn't he?"

"Ben? The best. He makes no secret of his lifestyle, but no one cares, here."

He grinned again. "Do you think he will seduce Renaldo?"

Clint shrugged. "Why would I care? They're both adults."

"Strange as it is to me, I have to agree. Who cares? It's their lives."

Clint waved to Manny, who came to the rear deck in his boat. He had his wife with him. Clint introduced everyone. Manny got along very well with Jim. Clint excused himself and went outside to call Manolo. He told him about the deal and gave him a lot of information. Manolo said he had met Jaime, once. He seemed to be Okay. There wasn't a tiny hint of anything that would concern the agencies Manolo worked with about him. He had buildings full of art and jewels, but it was, every piece, so far as they could tell, perfectly above-board. He inherited so much and was into so many companies that it wasn't even possible to know what he was worth.

"He's worth a fortune, as a person – and I'm not impressed by the money and all that kind of crap," Clint replied. "What do you want from me? This isn't gratis."

"I wanted you to know who we're dealing with. The chest Sergio found, the real pirate's treasure, was

Jaime's. He doesn't care about the loot, but he doesn't want any mention of him connected to it or to anything else, here. He's not involved, Manolo."

"Why does he think he will be?"

"Because the chest with the money was put there by a pirate called Cutter. Cutter was the original Cano. The original Serrano was called Fire Eyes – actually, the second. El Tiburón was the first, but he wasn't as successful, as a pirate. The two families do not like one another. They are very different kinds of people."

"From the same life, one is a pillar of society and one is the same kind of scum. One ascended, the other merely descended. A good argument for the genetic imperative producing the strong potential, but not the direction."

"Sheesh! You've been talking to Dave!"

They chatted a moment, then Clint went back inside. An attractive girl from Denmark was obviously very interested in Clint. Manny said, "Gina?"

"Ah! Miss Halverson will be back, from time to time, as a friend, but she will not long remain interested in the exotic detective," Jim warned. "I knew her father, quite well. I have met Gina on several occasions. She is a very independent person. It is good that she will have the wealth that will come, but she will spend much of it very quickly. She wants to know the entire world, not just Panamá and Colombia and Texas. She will expect Clint to understand that there are no chains. On either."

They soon decided to call it a night. Jim was invited to stay on Isla Colón with Manny's family. He said a couple of days for a vacation would be most welcome, at this juncture. He called Renaldo to say he had to fend for himself for a day or two. He could stay on the avion or at a hotel. Clint said he had a spare room. He said maybe he'd stay at Clint's. There was a pause. He said he would stay at Ben's. Jim giggled.

When he hung up, Manny asked what the giggle was about. "Oh, I was wondering if Ben would seduce my son. I would suggest the question is answered!" They had a laugh about it, then went their separate ways. Clint went to a couple of places with Inga, then she stayed at his place for the night.

It was a beautiful day when he awoke, in the morning. He slipped out of bed and fixed coffee and an omelette. He went out to his deck for the breakfast. He waved to Judi, watering her orchids on her own deck. It was just 6:30, a bit late for Clint. He then went inside to work with his computer. Inga got up a little after nine.

Clint made an omelette for her, she went swimming off his deck, then came in to dress and they went into town. She soon met her friends, who had been worried about her. She didn't tell them she had other arrangements for the night. She introduced Clint to them and said he was showing her around Bocas Town. They couldn't go to the mainland, like they had planned, because of the water taxi situation. Clint spent until noon, showing them all around, then they decided they would take the bus to Boca del Drago for the afternoon. Clint said he had to get to work and said goodbyes. Manolo called to say Jaime could relax. It seemed the Cano family had the word that Serrano would discreetly have every single one of them fingered if they so much as mentioned they'd ever heard his name.

Well, that seemed to settle things.

Clint had another good night, this time without stay-over company. He saw Ben and Renaldo twice the following day, from a distance to just wave to. Gina called and said she wouldn't be back to Bocas for awhile. She had a trip to Paris and London and a few other places planned. Clint talked to Jim and Manny on the phone. Clint told him his problem was solved and done. He could relax and enjoy. They had been out fishing for most of the day. Jim hadn't been able to relax so much in years. He had forgotten too much of what made life worthwhile. He would visit. Often.

Clint and Judi took Clint's boat to Almirante for some shopping. Stuff was getting in short supply on Bocas.

Clint had a good meal, at home. He was a good cook who liked things different from restaurant fare, a lot of the time. He made a good old-fashioned Yankee pot roast with the vegetables he brought back from Almirante. He worked a bit on the computer and got to bed early. In the morning Jim came in to say he was heading back to Colombia. Renaldo was going to stay for a week or so with Ben. Jim seemed worried, so Clint shrugged and called Ben.

"Ben, Jim is getting worried about Renaldo. Not against or anything, but he has to know."

Ben laughed. "Tell him Renaldo is definitely not gay. It's just new and different. I'm going to take advantage of that. He's a dream of a man."

It was on speaker. Jim heard and sighed, then giggled. "That's something I never experienced. It would seem I have led a very sheltered life. The youth are so much freer, now. It would be my instinct to stop it, even before now."

"Then he would wonder about it even more and would eventually get involved with a much different type than Ben."

"Ah! The – what do you call it – forbidden fruit."

Ben said he might be a fruit, but definitely not forbidden. He hung up.

"I greatly envy the wealth of friends you have, Clint. I have noted that these people really *like* and respect you. I can only hope their respect for me is genuine.

"I will return to my duties and leave my son and heir in the capable hands of Ben and my privacy in your own capable hands. I am proud to call you friend!"

Dangerous Curves

What to do today?

Clint Faraday, retired detective from Florida, now residing in Bocas del Toro, Panamá, sighed, stretched, took a sip of the special coffee, and leaned on the wood rail of his deck. The bay was peaceful and pleasant, today. He looked over to see Judi Lum, his only neighbor with a view of his deck, watering her orchids. She wagged a finger at him and waved. He didn't bother to put on anything until he decided what he was going to do. He went fishing and diving yesterday. He had his computer work done. He didn't feel like doing anything but laze around. He'd do that.

He put his coffee on the rail and dove into the cool water for a quick swim to loosen up, climbed on deck again, finished the coffee and went in to rinse and put on shorts. He'd go into town and sit around, gossiping a bit. The talk was mostly about the stupid strike against the water taxis and such. The negativity against the union was growing by leaps and bounds. This would, if the people had any sense at all, damage the union for years to come. These tactics had always led to grief in the states so long ago that people had forgotten most of it. Now it was here.

Don't think about it. People are collectively stupid. They always will be. A bunch of thugs and worse would make a lot of money and the people would be that much further behind. Tourism would be hurt.

The comp dinged that he had e-mail. Probably advertisements.

Clint went in and clicked on the message. It wasn't e-mail, it was a chat. He answered that he was available. Gossip here was as good as at The Grill, usually.

"Twistedgrip17"? Who was that?

"You got audio?" came on the screen.

Clint clicked on the audio circuit. He had been paying for it for months, but had never bothered to use it.

"Yeah?" he asked.

"I met you in Las Tablas, about a year and a half ago. You were working on that phony gold mine scheme?"

"Phony mine?"

"It was sulfur that was supposed to be silver or something."

"Oh. A sulfur dome that was supposed to be oil," Clint said. "Sort of stupid. Anyone who ever read a sonic recording could tell the difference, not to mention that oil isn't found in that kind of place."

"Whatever. I need a bit of help. Something is strange here – well, not here. In Santiago, but I came here to get away from it. You're a detective, so maybe you can find out what the hell is going on!"

"Tell me about it," Clint suggested.

"Oh! I'm Ed Granger. The overweight ex-boxer from Arkansas. I didn't stop to think that you wouldn't have the foggiest idea of who I am.

"It's odd things that happen. I got some weird e-mails and a few letters in my box. I have a P.O. box.

"Listen. I'll pay for a ticket. You can fly out to meet me in Santiago, tonight? You can see what happened and what kinds of things come in the mail and so forth. I also had my brakes fail in my truck in the mountains. If I wasn't such a good driver, I'd be dead.

"That wouldn't be so strange, because a lot of brakes fail in those mountains. They get damned hot coming down with a load.

"There was some kind of thing on the master. I don't know what it did, but think it blocked the fluid, or something. I don't know how it was timed."

That was getting interesting! "I'll catch the four o'clock," Clint promised.

Clint put a few things in a bag and made a curry for lunch, then met with friends to gossip awhile, then went to the airport at three. The ticket was there. He boarded at a quarter to four and was in Santiago at ten to five.

Ed Granger wasn't overweight, except in his own mind. He was still hard-muscled and in good health at fifty two. He had a very slight paunch that he was working to lose. He had the scars and such of a boxer. His nose was a small bit slanted toward the left. His ears showed the normal damage of a heavyweight. His hair was thick and mostly black, with some greying. He was affable and nervous. He was with a Panamanian girl. She was very goodlooking, in a cheap sort of way. She had a shape that was on the edge of being overdone. Granger introduced her as Toña. He said he was the novio of her sister, Nilsa.

Clint wondered what Nilsa looked like.

They went to the Bocas del Toro Hotel, where a room was already paid for Clint to stay. Toña went to the almacen, then would go back to the finca. Nilsa would come to pick Ed up about six. They could go to a restaurant or whatever.

Clint put what little he'd brought in his room. He and Ed went to a trucking company that Ed owned, with a couple of partners. All of them had their own trucks, and drove them, plus, they would hire local haulers for anything more than they could handle. They weren't getting rich, but were comfortable. Ed liked to make long hauls. He had the eighteen wheeler rig.

He showed Clint his truck, then went into his private office and took a device from the safe, there (explaining that anything not locked up disappeared). It was a simple solenoid with a battery and little comp board.

Clint looked it over and noted the imprint on the circuit board.

"It's a cell phone board. The way it works is that the number to the SIM is called, which sends a pulse to the solenoid. What was the solenoid hooked to?" Clint asked, when Ed gave him the look about saying it was from a celular. He took a piece of the tape off the board and showed him the SIM card. It was a Mas Movil, so Clint carefully took the chip out and put it into one of his phones, then punched the number of his other phone. It rang and he gave Ed the number on the ID. Ed shook his head.

Ed said there wasn't anything attached, that he could find.

"It was the truck out there?"

"Yeah."

Clint went out and looked at the spot the device had been attached, after asking the secretary, Donna, a few questions. She didn't seem to know anything.

There was a small piece of nylon fishing line hanging from a brake line below and behind the unit. He fished it out to find a strange shaped piece of metal on the end. He shrugged.

Ed checked it, studied the hexagonal hole on one end, then slipped it down to fasten on the end bolt of a tiny valve.

"I'll be damned! It opens the pressure end on the calibrator nut. It adjusted the pressure to zero, so the brakes didn't work. When it came off, the valve closed itself on a little spring. As long as I tried to use the brakes, it made them not work. When I let it just stand for a minute, the spring readjusted the release. If you hadn't found that string, we could never know what happened!"

"The string and wrench were supposed to fall off on the road. It caught on a brake line behind ... because you were moving. The wind stream blew it back and it wrapped on," Clint said. "Clever."

"Can we find who ... I guess not." Ed said. "I want to know why anyone would do that!"

"It's possible we can find that, easily enough," Clint replied. "They handled the circuit board."

"Yeah! And you only touched the edges of the SIM card! Neat!"

Clint carefully removed the card from his phone, by the edges. He dumped a fine powder from a vial in his pocket onto it, then lightly blew most of the powder away, leaving what appeared to be a thumb print showing on the card. He took some Scotch Tape to lift the print.

"Now we have to find whose phone it was, though I figure it was stolen or bought for this one purpose. We might have the print of a clerk, on the card."

He slid the battery off the card and checked it, but it had been wiped.

"Now we have to learn why any of this damned crap is happening," he explained. "I'll try to trace that tomorrow morning. You can give me some background tonight."

They went to dinner. Nilsa was much like her sister, who came with her and kept making a play for Clint, who wasn't interested in the type. Clint met Andres Gomez, one of the partners.

After a decent meal of chicken, done rotisserie style, Clint went to the finca, a two hectare plot with a nice house, very close into town. He learned what little Ed could tell him.

Ed had come to Panamá when he retired as a boxing coach. He was a truck driver for a time in the states, and wanted to establish something to do here. He was not allowed, as non-Panamanian, to drive, commercially, but there is an easy way around almost anything, in Panamá. He was an employee of his own corporation and could drive, so long as he had a Panamanian driver with him. He had hired a man with a license as a copilot and helper. On timed runs, he could drive a few hours, then his copilot would drive a few. They could make a trip that took most of the night, that way.

Interesting. He said Nilsa and Toña set the deal up.

"I want to see the corporation certification papers," Clint demanded. "I think I see what's going on."

Ed looked surprised. He took a copy from the safe. He spent some time studying the contract, then said he could almost figure it. He had to check a few things, but Ed was to be very careful. He then went back to the hotel, where he talked a few minutes with the woman running the place. She knew the Gomez family. Nilsa and Toña were sisters.

And Andres is their brother, Clint thought.

He went across the street to the popular little bar, where he talked with a few people. Two Indios came in and Clint went to speak with them. He introduced himself in their dialect. That identified him as a friend. He talked awhile with them before asking if they had ever worked for the trucking company. They hadn't, but knew some who had. They were alright. Some of the people there treated them like people, but one was an ass. The women who hung around were worse. They would like the work, but not if they had to put up with the shit.

"Yeah, that Andres person and his sisters," Clint said. "I heard." They agreed, but they didn't think they were sisters. Just cousins.

Same difference, so far as Clint was concerned.

He went back to the hotel and studied the corporation papers, very closely. They were fairly standard through the first four pages and on the last, but had a clause on page five stating that an insurance policy was to be kept on all partners, payable to the others in case of death, and that all assets become the property of the survivors. Exactly what he expected.

He got a good night's sleep and went out to breakfast to find the secretary, Donna, waiting there. She said she was worried about Ed, that she maybe knew something, but she was scared, for her own sake, if she told.

"I'll see that no one knows it was you who tells me anything," Clint promised.

She took a deep breath, then said, "Some of my friends, indigenos, used to work for Andres, when he owned another trucking company with a man called Sergio Bannister. He was Panamanian, on his mother's side, and gringo, on his father's. He died in an accident, where his truck went off a mountain on a dangerous curve. They don't know why he was going so much too fast, coming down the mountain.

"That is where Andres got the money and truck to go into the business here. There was a big insurance policy no one knew anything about, or something.

"Well, Ed had the same thing happen, but he knows how to handle it. It did damage the truck, a little, but nothing serious.

"Nilsa and Toña were on the company papers with Bannister. Now the same thing almost happens with Mr. Ed. Andres said to not say anything about anything to you, because he doesn't trust you – but he never saw you until you came to the yard. I know that, because he asked who you were and what you wanted when you talked to me."

"Thanks, Donna. I knew some of it, so you didn't really tell me anything, except for one thing. I'll say you don't know anything to tell, if anyone asks.

"One thing, the sisters aren't on the corporation papers. I've read them."

"It's a different contract. They made it when Mr. Ed said he would live with Nilsa."

"That ties up another important little detail. Thanks, Donna."

She nodded, said thanks, and left. Clint called Ed. He asked why Ed didn't tell him there was a separate contract that put the Gomez sisters into the corporation. He said there wasn't. He would never sign that kind of thing. He might not be particularly bright. That didn't mean he was abjectly stupid! You did *not* let that kind of person onto a corporation. They could get a crooked lawyer and steal the whole thing from you.

At nine, Clint went to the records department and checked over the contracts registered in the corporation name. It was there, so he paid the three dollars for a certified copy and called Ed to meet him at the MacDonalds. He walked over, five blocks, and waited about twenty minutes for Ed to come in, accompanied by Nilsa.

He didn't say anything, just tossed the contract on the table. Nilsa squealed, then tried to look innocent.

"I'm a detective. You had to guess that I'd find that as soon as I came here."

She said it wasn't her idea. That Andres had suggested it, so she would be taken care of if there was an accident or something.

"But you knew the signature is forged, didn't you?" Ed asked, through his teeth. She didn't answer.

"Better to talk to me now than an hour from now, I flat goddamned well guarantee you!" he snarled.

"I didn't know anything!" she cried. "It was Andres! I didn't know the signature wasn't yours! He said it was!"

"Is that also true of Bannister?" Clint asked. She looked scared, then turned and ran from the place.

"I'll be damned!" Ed said, hotly. "So she was setting me up to knock me over for the company, all along?"

"And the insurance policy," Clint agreed.

"What damned insurance policy? If I get hurt or killed in the truck? That's only fifty grand. The truck's worth a hell of a lot more than that!

"Oh! They'd get the truck, too."

"No. The five hundred grand life insurance policy on you. Double indemnity. It's on the corporation papers."

"So. I chase a hot piece of ass like that and go over a curve on the mountain and she gets rich," Ed said. "God, I'm stupid, sometimes!"

"There's more than one definition to the phrase, ´dangerous curves´," Clint pointed out.

"Okay. What do we do now? I've had enough experience with the law here to know we can't prove anything, with what we have. Maybe about that other guy you said they did this kind of thing to?"

"Not likely. I'll handle it. Would your other partner have anything to do with it?"

"No. He's a Panamanian who put up money to help me. He wasn't going to be on anything, but I put him on it."

"It's a damned good thing he's on it. When the corporation goes into his control, you're covered with having a Panamanian as a major partner. You can find any Panamanian to be your third partner when Andres has to resign – for personal reasons."

"You suggest somebody."

Clint thought, then said, "Maybe tonight I'll come up with two partners, who might even work for the corporation. They're Indigenos, so you get some breaks there, to add to it. It'll damned well mean you can haul stuff onto the comarcas. I'll go speak with Andres – unless he's already run."

Ed nodded. He said he had to go home and throw a couple of whores off his property. Clint told him to watch his back.

"And all around. I'll go armed. I have a permit. The pistol's in the truck."

"Check it before you get into a spot where you have to use it."

"*That's* automatic."

Clint went to the hotel, then across the street to ask who the Indios were from last night, and where could he find them?

"Huh! How much did they take?" the bartender asked. "You're a gringo. You better learn not to trust Indios."

"They didn't take anything from me. I've lived among them. I know that most of them are damned good people. They aren't bigots, though they're certainly the ones with the right!"

He turned red. He said they worked for the cattle brokers, most of the time. Clint went to find them. They were working with heavy sacks of grain, so he waited. They came to him soon. He told them they were going to be officers in a corporation, so he had to know their names and cedula numbers.

They thought it was a great joke. Would they be Andres' boss?

"No. He won't be around, anymore. Neither will the two puta cousins."

They laughed, gave him the information, and went back to their work, laughing about being corporate heads. They didn't really believe him, but also thought it would be true, because he was a friend, so wouldn't lie to them – unless it was a joke. Wait and see.

Clint went to the company. Andres was in his office, reading a copy of the contract.

"It's void. I can bring up Bannister. You'll spend the next ten years under investigation, where every least move you make will be noted. You'd be smart to sign off the corporation. I might use your own methods to see you out. I have no compunction from using the rules you made on you."

"I've got everything I own in this place! I can't just leave it!"

"You have what you got by knocking Bannister over. You never deserved a single centavo of that, anyhow."

"That wasn't my idea! It was Nilsa!"

"Funny. She said the same about you," Clint said. "You have today and tomorrow. Be out of Santiago before dawn, the day after tomorrow."

He got up and left. Clint went back to the hotel. Toña was waiting. He sighed and asked her what she wanted – that she wasn't going to get.

"I wanted to explain that I wasn't part of anything. I like Ed. It was Andres."

"He said it was you. It was all of you. Don't be so stupid as to think you can get around me by shaking your ass. I know fifty women who outclass you."

"How am I supposed to make a living here, after this! It's a lie!" she wailed. "Mentira, mentira, mentira!"

"Then the smart thing would be to go somewhere else," Clint suggested. "You will definitely not be able to pull this kind of crap around here, again. If you try it somewhere else, I'll see that the policía have the particulars to make it come back and slap you in the puss."

She started to say something nasty, thought about it, then simply walked out. Clint went back inside, cleaned up, and walked around town for awhile. Santiago is as different from David or Bocas as they are from Santiago.

He stayed until Andres and the sisters caught the bus for Panamá City, then headed to David for a couple of days, then on to Bocas. In Bocas, he spent as couple of days doing little or nothing.

He was getting bored. The detective business in Florida was mostly boring. Here, it held excitement. He was more involved in dangerous situations, here.

He was in The Pirate, having a couple of beers with friends, when a girl with a truly exceptional figure came in and gave him an interested look. He remembered what he recently said to Ed about dangerous curves.

"What the hell!" he said to no one.

It was a great night.

Clint Faraday, PI, Ret'd. stretched his back and made a noise. He had been sitting at the damned comp for hours, but was finally caught up. He checked to find it was after five, so no fishing or anything today. He stripped and dove into the bay from his deck, swam until his muscles and bones were back to normal, then went inside, rinsed and dressed for town. He went to El Ultimo Refugio (Or just Refugio's) for a great meal, talked with a number of the locals, listened to his nutty musician friend for awhile, then headed toward the center of town. As he was rounding the curve by the ferry docks, a taxi came close enough to brush his hand. He threatened to pull the asshole out of the cab and kick his ass from one end of the street to the other, if he ever came that close again.

Night driving was about the same in Bocas as day driving. Taxi drivers were, famously, assholes. They thought it was cute to see how close they could come. If it had been more daylight, he would have given Clint a much wider berth. Clint wasn't known for good humor, in that kind of situation.

He went on, stopping at La Iguana, but it was too early for much there, so he went to El Toro Loco for a couple of beers. He met some people he knew from a previous trip they made to Bocas. They chatted awhile, Clint caught them up on the local situation, then they split up, Clint going on to The Plank, they going, because Clint had recommended it, to Refugio's.

Not much at The Plank, so he went to The Rip Tide, just a bit farther along. Neil and Cathy were serving exceptional food tonight. Clint half wished he had waited, but there are several good restaurantes in Bocas.

He was there most of the time. He could come here tomorrow.

Neil said there was trouble brewing. A taxi had hit a gringo on a bicycle the night past. She was claiming it was on purpose. She wasn't hurt badly, because she saw it coming just in time. She got partly out of the way.

Clint tended to agree that it was on purpose. If she had time to see the taxi coming, the taxi had time to avoid hitting her. If she was trying to get aside, the taxi had to go more toward her to have hit her, at all.

Nothing would be done. She was a tourist. She would be gone in a couple of days. They would make a little noise about it and drop it when she left. Sooner or later, someone was going to really get hurt, then there would be enough "I should have ... s" going around to make you puke.

Clint went home to bed, about midnight.

In the morning, Clint got up and decided to go to Chiriqui Grande and return the following day. He took his boat to make the trip, enjoyed the stay, and returned. He went around town, this time, eating dinner at The Rip Tide and ending up at Refugio's, where he met a girl from France. To make a long story short, she spent the night at his place.

The next day, he went fishing with Manny and Dave, for most of the day, then went around town for awhile. Sergio, police jefe, found him at La Iguana at about ten thirty. He said a taxi had hit a woman who was in critical condition.

"It had to happen," Clint said. "You should crack down on those assholes."

"We try, but that's traffic's department. There are only two traffic cops here. They miss almost everything," Sergio said. "The reason I felt I should get you involved is that she was hit a couple of nights ago, but not hurt, badly. She claimed she was hit, deliberately. It looks like she was right."

"What does the driver say?"

"We don't know who it was. A couple of people saw it from the sidewalk toward town and it was going away from them. They couldn't describe it, except to say it was a taxi, like most of them you see here."

"Then it was deliberate. When can I talk to her?"

"In the morning."

"Sergio, put a guard on her."

"I did. I also made it plain that no one was to know which room she's in."

Clint nodded.

"She can talk until she gets tired. That will be very quickly," Dr. Avanzas warned. "You will leave at that time until she recovers better. She is still in dangerous condition. We do not have the more modern facilities or equipment here. We're hardly more than first aid, and a large percent of the staff are qualified only in a small area."

Clint agreed. He went to her room. He sat by the bed until she stirred and looked at him. He introduced himself and said he wanted to know what was going on. Who, why – and anything else she could tell him.

She didn't know who or why. She couldn't tell him anything, except this was the third try. They were getting better at it.

"First time?"

"In Panamá City. A car came flying around a corner as I was crossing. It would have hit me dead center, if I hadn't heard it and jumped onto the center break. He just kept going. There was no license plate on the car is why I didn't put it to another night driver who shouldn't be allowed to drive, even in the daylight."

"When was that?"

"The night of August six. Right on the corner before the Europa Hotel."

"I know about the two here. Are you positive there were no attempts before August six?"

"No. I was in town only since the evening, six o'clock, of the fifth. I hadn't gone anywhere, except for the Hotel California and the restaurant there. I walked around the one block there for a few minutes before I went to the hotel and to bed. Nothing happened." She yawned, said, "sorry," and dropped to sleep. Clint left. As soon as he was outside, he called Sergio and said he'd be there in five minutes.

"Sergio, what happened in Panamá on August fifth, around eight o'clock to eleven? In the area of the Hotel California?"

He checked the sheets. "Other than ... nothing, really. A couple of muggings, but farther down on Via España. Some drug dealer was stabbed, but that was down closer to the X-zone." (The X-zone is where there are a number of X-rated movies and porno/sex toy shops)

"Something went down there. It had to be. She was only in Panamá a few hours. That's the only place she went."

"If it had been the fifth, at the airport, she might have seen something. Some bigshot was almost assassinated, or something. It was about the time the Continental flight came in from Miami."

"Hmm. Why would they single her out?" Clint wondered. "She was just there by chance. She didn't note anything happening." Sergio shrugged. He said it must be something else.

"It's the only thing I have. I'm going to Panamá, I think. Get someone pushed. I can just make the flight, if

I hurry. I have enough cash that I can buy a set of clothes there, if I need a change."

Sergio called the airport and said there was a seat available, but Clint had to get there in seven minutes. They wouldn't hold the flight long. The police truck was outside. Sergio said to get Clint to Aeroperlas in five minutes or less.

They did.

It was drizzling a bit in Panamá City, nothing unusual, this time of the year. Clint went directly to the Hotel California. Sergio had called and asked for a room for him. There wasn't one available. They arranged for him to stay at the Europa. It was close enough that it wouldn't matter.

He went to the California for dinner. He had the shrimp spaghetti, which he particularly liked, there. No one knew anything. That was the place to find information of a certain type. It wasn't there. Clint knew who to ask.

The Europa had some bigshots staying there, who left about the time the Continental flight got to Tucumen. One was a main man in the government, here. In immigration. The other two were from Colombia and Venezuela. The Venezuelan was almost assassinated at the airport, but a tip saved him.

Interesting. Clint called the Panamá Policía to find his good friend wasn't there for another week. He was on his vacation. A Capitan Lincoln said he knew Clint's story and reputation with the department. He would be granted the same cooperation he was used to, there. He didn't know much about the Velasquez assassination attempt. Someone knew all about it beforehand, because a tip was called in, describing exactly what was going down. A woman who called from an airport payphone.

She made another call, later, to tell them a man called El Tigre was the almost-assassin. She called from a payphone near the Hotel California. Across the Via España, as a matter of fact. She knew Jimenez would be with them.

"Jimenez?" Clint asked.

"Immigration biggy, here. Crooked as a snake, but I didn't say that. We haven't *yet* been able to catch him. The other one was Gardina, from Colombia."

"Why would they think someone who just arrived on a plane from Miami would ... I don't know enough," Clint complained. "Well, at least, I have a starting point."

He thought a moment, after hanging up, then went downstairs to the lobby to talk to the staff. None of them had a clue. He decided to check up on Velasquez and El Tigre. A call to Manolo, a friend who was an agent for Interpol who knew most of what was going on. He said Velasquez was into oil or something and El Tigre could be any of seven people who were known by the name. What else was he mixed up in?

"Something to do with immigration, I'd say," Clint answered. "Jimenez."

"It's big, then. Probably, El Tigre would be Samuel Gortas. Him or one other ... no, not big enough. It'll be Gortas. Anybody else involved on their end?"

"Gardina. From Colombia."

"Um-hm. Gortas. What's it about?"

"A woman in Bocas is to be hit. She happened to be on a plane from Miami that landed not long before the assassination attempt. A woman called from the airport with a tip, then called again from near the Hotel California. They put two and two together and got seven and three quarters."

"They tend to do that. Good luck!"

Clint thought a minute more. He didn't know much. What could be the connection that would make an assassination attempt among that group? All he had to work on was that Jimenez was in immigration. That would mean someone was in Panamá who was of interest to the other two – or they were trying to arrange for someone to come to Panamá who was persona non grata to someone here.

Logic: Jimenez wouldn't have much influence in getting anyone in. He was watched. Someone was here who didn't want to be found by those two.

What could be the connection between those two?

He shook his head. He said he would stay the night in the Europa, then head back to Bocas.

He was out until nearly midnight before he went back to the hotel and up to his room. He got a telephone message. A woman. "Boquete. Two years." She hung up.

Interesting. He would change his plans to go to David and Boquete. He hoped he had a clear enough clue in that.

He slept well, then left in the morning on the bus. That would throw the man following him off, a bit. He could be going to David or on to Bocas. From David, he could go anywhere he liked.

He thought a bit, then called Manolo.

"Does El Tigre stand about six two, has longish black hair, about two twenty? Flashy jewelry, smokes cigars. The small ones. Big diamond ring and pierced ear."

"Uh-huh. He following you?"

"He was. I sort of messed up his head when I caught the bus."

"He'll beat you to Santiago to see if you get off or go on to David. Be very careful. He's very professional, usually. He was rushed, I suppose, so missed. Maybe he's figured he was after the wrong one. That means you've figured something. You're now the dangerous party, in a manner of speaking."

Clint talked another minute, then relaxed. He rode to Penonomé, got off, waited for the second following bus, two hours later, and went on to David. He didn't get off the bus in Santiago. No one checked inside. El Tigre would have to figure he never intended to go to David. Now he would have to wonder where he did go.

He got into David at the rush hour. It was easy to get off the bus in Las Lomas and take a taxi into David. He went to El Poderosa and bought a clean change of clothes, then went to the Pensión Costa Rica, where he took a room.

He had to worry about one other thing: he could lead someone to exactly the person he didn't want them led to. He had to be very careful.

He went to Poderosa to buy another set of clothes in a quite different style. He would use a disguise.

A sort of gawky Panameño with rather too long hair left the Costa Rice, wearing a backpack. Lee, the owner, noticed him and started to say something, paused, then did.

"What's going on here? You come out, but you never went in. You look very different."

"Hi, Lee. I'm trying not to lead some people to a person they intend to kill."

"Faraday? I'll be damned! That's a damned good disguise!"[a]

"If anyone knows I'm here, I went to Pedrigal. I should be back anytime after an hour or so. I may go to a mariscos place for dinner. This is Pete Somebody you're talking to, now. You can give Edith a name to give out if anyone asks if there's anyone who looks like this staying."

"Okay. Be careful. If they're looking to kill someone else and you get in the way, it could be you *and* someone else."

Clint nodded. He went to the bus station, got the Bugaba bus, got the Boquete bus in Bugaba, and was there in an hour, strolling around the parque.

Here was Boquete. What about the two years?

Something happened to someone two years ago, or there was someone who had been here two years.

He went to the coffee shop/restaurante at the back corner and asked about some friends, which gave him an idea. He called Robert Fellon, who had been there for about six years. They met at the restaurante to talk. Clint asked about anyone who had been there two years who deliberately remained out of sight.

"Maybe the Johnsons. Maybe those Cortez people," he replied. "Johnson is from Ohio. He's about sixty five. He's just antisocial, I think. Sour disposition, and everything's because the states have gone straight to hell because of the liberal commies, or something.

"Cortez is here from Costa Rica. They're just disliked, for some reason. He tries to be more arrogant than some of the gringos here. He rubs you the wrong way ... how about someone who is very much in sight, but seems to me to be in disguise?"

"How so?"

"Carlos Vega. He came here with a real knockout woman, Flora Rios, and was black-haired and clean-shaven. She was and is a Latina, with eyes that promise you passion and heaven. She wore really sexy clothes when they got here, but was dressing 'way down, within a week. He grew a bushy moustache and wears clothes that make him look fatter than he is. He started wearing glasses two days after they got here. I've looked through them at a newspaper they were laying on. They're not magnifying or distorting anything. I've seen him reading a newspaper, suddenly realizing he doesn't have them on, and puts them on. He smoked cigars, constantly, the first couple of days. He's stopped smoking, altogether. Sometimes you think he's not Spanish, for some reason. They go to the clubs and drink cokes. Once in awhile, a beer. At a celebration, a couple of months ago, he drank a Chivas on the rocks. He was getting the second when she got him aside. He stopped drinking anything. They left, after a little while.

"The change in looks. He'd lightened his hair a bit. She cut her long hair and went for a pageboy look. It doesn't suit her. She had beautiful hair, down almost to her waist. His hair was clipped very short, now it's almost shoulder length. You can tell he doesn't like it.

"Lots of things, you notice if you're around them for a couple of years, that most people would hardly notice, but I was a cop, back in Detroit."

"Purloined letters," Clint said. "Where can I find them?"

He pointed to the road up the mountain. "That big stucco place with the big white stone wall. Ostentatious. Like you said, purloined letters."

"Sometimes, the best way to hide is to be so close to the searcher's face he keeps pushing you aside to see what's behind you. Thanks, Bob."

He went out and to the road, walked up, and looked at the house, started to go in to knock on the door, changed his mind, and went back to the parque. He called Manolo and gave him the descriptions. Nothing. He called Manny, ditto. He called a friend in Colombia, Jaime. Nothing.

They weren't jewel or art thieves. They weren't mob-connected. They weren't involved in drugs. What? Clint was sure they were it.

One thing to do. He went back to David and to the pensión to become Clint Faraday, again. There had been a call for him. Edith said he was in Pedrigal.

Okay. His follower knew Clint was in the pensión, but wasn't there earlier. He would be watching the place. Clint couldn't walk out, if he didn't first walk in.

Lee owned the whole quarter block. He was building a restaurant on the side street that could be entered through the pensión. Clint became himself and went through the little yard and into the restaurant. He scanned the street carefully outside, then casually strolled along the side of the building and in the front. Edith greeted him and said someone was looking for him. He nodded, and went back to his room, stayed about twenty minutes, then went out and to the little local restaurant across from the taxi stand and Romero's. Gortas came to sit at a table behind him. He got the plate and went to sit across from Gortas, who looked a bit surprised, then a bit more scared.

"Give!" Clint ordered. "Who are you looking for, and why? How were you ever so stupid as to involve the innocent tourist woman in your scheme?"

Gortas studied him for a minute, then grinned. "I would waste my time lying to you. I think you're a very dangerous hombre.

"I am sorry she became involved. The situation is very dangerous to some powerful people in three countries. It appeared she was the one person who could know too much about it. She is in no danger more. This I swear."

"You'll send her five thousand dollars and an apology," Clint stated. "If you ever do anything like that again, you won't survive the day. It'll be done in such a way you'll beg to end it. I'm not interested in this shit, beyond seeing that woman has things made as right as possible to her.

"I *am* curious." He waited a moment.

"It's about some people who were planning a robbery of a lot of emeralds a certain person who got them by the same tactics was holding in a vault. There was something else in the vault. Some very important information about some *very* important people. They got the information and a few of the emeralds, which they have now discreetly turned into cash, which is how we found who they are."

"The information is about people staying here in Panamá to hide from other people?"

"Si. And people in other countries who are hiding from people here. These people tend to spend inordinate time hiding."

"It's usually because they tried shortcuts to something they didn't really want," Clint said. "Are these hidden people hiding from others like them, or from more, shall we label them, legal situations?"

"Those people don't hide from legal situations. That is why so many sleazy lawyers are needed."

Clint grinned. He could like Gortas, if he wasn't what he was.

"If I return the information to you, will you stop the search for the ones who got it?"

"Him, yes. Her, no way! She's the type to use what she knows for blackmail. It will make a bad situation much worse."

"That is fact?" Clint stared hard into his eyes.

"This is not her first ... escapade. It is not her third."

Clint nodded. "Give me a cel number. Do *not* follow me. I'll see what I can do."

"Have you seen her?" Gortas asked, with a small smirk on his face.

"No."

"Ah-hah! 'Watch out for those soft shoulders and dangerous curves'," Gortas sang the old country song.

"So I've heard, from someone who has seen her. Often."

Gortas handed him a slip with a cel number on it. He left to head for the bus. Gortas wouldn't break the agreement.

He arrived in Boquete a bit after six, where he went to a good Mexican restaurant. He learned that the Vega man usually went out after eight. That was plenty of time, so he strolled up to in front of the house and yelled, "Buenas!" A man who had to be Vega came to the door and asked what he wanted.

"I want to try to keep you and the lovely lady from being killed. I'm Clint Faraday. I believe she called me with a cryptic message."

"Not her. Come on in."

Clint went in. Vega didn't waste words. "How can we get out of this damned mess?"

"I don't know if she can. You can.

"How could anyone be stupid enough to think they could blackmail people like those?"

There was a pause, then he nodded. "So that's how it came apart. I was wondering why they were so suddenly trying to kill us. That would be, to my thinking, the fastest way to have the information she holds distributed.

"I learned, two years ago, when we came here, that I was in a very bad situation because of her. I did not know what she was or her history. Then. I, quite frankly, wouldn't lift a finger to protect her. I need a way to protect myself *from* her!"

"She isn't here?"

"She went into town to purchase groceries. She wants to know if anyone was asking about us. She knows about the woman in Bocas.

"I am most sorry about that. My caller was thought to be her.

"Mr. Faraday, I want out of this! I tried to cause something that would allow me out. She is the one who was arranging for the assassination of Velasquez. He should be shot, but not by such as her."

"Why would she try to hit Velasquez?"

"He has much of the information she holds. He made it quite plain that he would have her eliminated as a problem, if he finds her. She is very good at hiding in plain sight."

"I figured that. So did another person here.

"Is the information here?"

"In a safe in her room. Yes."

"All of it?"

"It is there with all the copies. She couldn't find a way to place the copies where she could feel secure about them."

"Can you call her?"

"Certainly."

"Call her. When I do certain things, act like it's real. First, tell her there are two men in the house. You think one is a man you saw in Panamá City."

He went to the desk phone and called a cell number. When she answered, he said what Clint suggested in a whispered, panicky voice. Clint slammed a nearby door against the wall. Clint acted like he was throwing a fist. Vega grunted and dropped the receiver. Clint knocked the phone off the table. Vega made some more grunts. Clint turned the table over onto the phone and made a lot of noise, then picked up the phone and said, "Te matarse, puta!" and hung up.

Vega grinned at him. "What now?"

Clint took out his cell and called Gortas. "The stuff is in a safe in her room. Get it! She won't be back here.

"Oh. Boquete. Hill road, fourth house. The ostentatious one. Her room's ... (he raised his eyebrows at Vega) North corner. Carved teak door. Vega is out of it, so long as nothing else happens where he involves himself."

Gortas grunted and hung up.

"Get whatever you can't do without and let's get the hell out of here. They'll have someone close, so we don't have much time."

He said, "She'll be somewhere she can watch the place, pretty fast. She'll sneak in to see if the stuff's still here."

"There's a back way out?"

"Yeah. She'll watch that, more than the front ... which means we can go out the front, if we stay right against the wall. She won't be able to see. She knows, if someone is in here, they had to come in from in back, somehow. The security in front is damned good. The laundry room is the only place they could get in."

Clint asked where the laundry room was. He went back to wrench the door askew. It would look forced, from a distance. Vega grabbed a suitcase, threw a lot of things in, asked Clint to carry the briefcase he slid from under a chair in the dinning room. They slipped out the front door and along the wall to the corner.

They could be seen from the hill she would have to be on, if they crossed the intersection. Clint was looking around when a car stopped in front of the house and three burly men went to find the door open. Clint grinned at Vega, said, "It's done. She can run, but I doubt she can hide."

They walked across the intersection and down toward town, caught the last bus back to David, and went to the Costa Rica. In the morning, Vega caught a bus to Panamá City and Clint went back to Bocas. On the bus, the radio announced that a burglary in Boquete in a very wealthy area had resulted in the death of the woman who lived there. Her husband was missing. The blood on the scene indicated that he was probably also dead. The robbery seemed to be of a safe and all its contents that had been removed from the house.

Clint was trying to remember the words to that song Gortas sang a line of. *Watch Out for Those Soft Shoulders and Dangerous Curves*. Something about trouble and ruining your nerves, or something.

Too true.

C. D. Moulton's works are available on most major outlets as printed or e-books. CD writes the CD Grimes, PI, mysteries, the Det. Lt. Nick Storie mysteries, the Clint Faraday mysteries, the Flight of the Maita science fiction series, books on orchid culture and many others of many types. Mystery, adventure, intrigue, science fiction, humor, fantasy, paranormal, mild erotica, and factual.